PRAISE FOR OTHER WORKS BY FRÉDÉRIQUE MOLAY

"Frédérique Molay exhibits high standards of writing. Art and the meaning of life mix perfectly here, in a story that expresses a desire to love and believe in people."

—*Le Bien Public*

"*The 7th Woman* blends suspense and authentic police procedure with a parallel tale of redemption. Well-drawn characters and ratcheting tension won't let you put the book down. I read this in one sitting."

—Paris mystery writer Cara Black

"Frédérique Molay is the French Michael Connelly."

—Jean Miot, Agence France-Presse (AFP)

"*The 7th Woman* is a taut and terror-filled thriller. Frédérique Molay navigates French police procedure with a deft touch, creating a lightning-quick, sinister plot with twists and turns that kept me reading late and guessing to the very end. Inspector Nico Sirsky is every bit as engaging and dogged as Arkady Renko in *Gorky Park* and is sure to become a favorite with readers in the United States and around the world."

—*New York Times* bestselling author Robert Dugoni

"It's the kind of suspense that makes you miss your subway stop or turn off your phone."

—RTL

"A slick, highly realistic, and impeccably crafted thriller. Likeable characters, outstanding pacing, and unexpected plot twists that keep readers guessing throughout . . . an extraordinary, hard-hitting novel."

—*Foreword Reviews*

"Author Frédérique Molay does a superb job of building the suspense in overt and subtle ways . . . Don't pick this book up unless you're planning to read for a while because, I assure you, you won't be able to put it down."

—*Criminal Element*

"Procedural fans will appreciate the fresh take."

—*Booklist*

"It is a handsomely written and wonderfully translated Parisian police procedural that also will prowl your mind . . . The ugly parts are appalling, but Molay has the prowess to touch lightly upon them before exploring the horror seeping into the hardened police ranks."

—*Durango Herald*

"More chilling suspense from Frédérique Molay."

—*Metro*

"A sophisticated murder mystery . . . that twists, turns, and is stitched together by a gossamer thread."

—*Durango Herald*

"From the Paris setting to the autopsy scenes, Molay's descriptions add believable imagery to this page-turner mystery."

—*Foreword Reviews*

"Molay is just the ticket."

"This is a fine procedural, with a vividly evoked Paris setting, compelling characters, and plenty of suspense."

"With a little bit about art, and the history of Paris thrown in, this was an intelligent read that I particularly enjoyed."

"A story that the fans of quality crime fiction will surely enjoy."

"Molay can give CSI writers a run for their money . . . The book transported me to Paris."

LOOKING TO THE
WOODS

OTHER PARIS HOMICIDE MYSTERIES

LOOKING TO THE
WOODS

A PARIS HOMICIDE MYSTERY

FRÉDÉRIQUE MOLAY

TRANSLATED BY ANNE TRAGER AND LE FRENCH BOOK

Text copyright © 2016 Frédérique Molay
Translation copyright © 2017 Anne Trager & Le French Book
All rights reserved.

Previously published as *Copier n'est pas jouer* by Amazon Publishing in France in 2016. Translated from French by Anne Trager and Le French Book with the collaboration of Amy Richards, translation editor. First published in English by AmazonCrossing in 2016.

Published by AmazonCrossing, Seattle

www.apub.com

Amazon, the Amazon logo, and AmazonCrossing are trademarks of Amazon.com, Inc., or its affiliates.

ISBN-13: 9781503941625
ISBN-10: 1503941620

Cover design by Jeroen ten Berge

However well you feed the wolf,
he still looks to the woods.

—Russian proverb

1

He tied up the body with great care, closed the suitcase, and pulled out the handle. His breathing was calm now.

With the warm, husky voice of Norah Jones traveling through his earbuds, he had stared at his prey. Sweat trickled down his back. All his senses were aroused. He quivered and felt dizzy.

Terrified, she had tried to fight back. But what could she have done? He was six feet tall, with the broad shoulders of an athlete. He covered her mouth and crushed her with all his weight. Then he grabbed the knife. He read the fear in her eyes, followed by capitulation. She knew she was going to die. There was no other outcome.

How could he possibly go on living without this kind of thrill?

Killing was so simple in the end. Child's play.

2

Sunday, May 5

Nico pulled Caroline closer, savoring the moment of bliss under the disheveled sheet. Even now, his desire for her remained as powerful as the first time they made love.

Caroline tucked her body into his. He felt himself growing aroused, but before he could act on it, she giggled and slapped him lightly on the thigh.

"That's enough, Inspector. Time to get up and get dressed. We have things to do today—a nice long walk and a picnic ahead of us."

"Just a few more minutes," he pleaded. As he began nuzzling her neck, his phone rang.

Nico and Caroline groaned in unison.

"No . . ." she said.

Nico gave her an apologetic look. "You know I have to take it."

"I know."

Five minutes later, he was in his car, his siren wailing and the blue gumdrop on the roof flashing like a dance-floor strobe. The traffic parted for him, and chief of police Nico Sirsky floored the gas pedal while Seal's "Crazy" blared from the speakers.

Nico knew he had to be crazy to be able to turn away from his loved ones—their laughter and joie de vivre—to do his job day in and day out. He had pried himself from Caroline's arms for yet another rotting body. Why? Why did he continue to subject himself to this? When he was younger, he thought he could save the world. But today? People killed for no reason at all. They killed as if it were a game.

Seal's rich, honest voice, the slamming of the bass guitar, and the throbbing of the keyboard served to focus his energy.

"We've got a body," Commander David Kriven had said on the phone. "She's being prepped for autopsy right now. Professor Vilars won't start without you."

Professor Armelle Vilars was the coroner and head of the Paris Medical Examiner's Office.

"Is Vidal there?"

Captain Pierre Vidal was the crime scene investigator on Kriven's team. The famed Paris Criminal Investigation Division at 36 Quai des Orfèvres had twelve teams, with six elite investigators on each, each one of whom had a specific skill set and role.

"He's still at the scene on the Square du Temple, where they found the girl. Plassard's running the show there."

Captain Franck Plassard was Kriven's right-hand man.

"Did the local precinct officers make a fuss?"

"Nope, they're cool in the third arrondissement. Handed the case right over."

Kriven was silent for a moment.

"Kriven? Are you okay?"

"Chief, prepare yourself. It's sick."

◆　◆　◆

Nico strode through the lobby, with its polished wood floors, white walls, and busts of past medical examiners. French doors led to a small patio with flowers and a fountain. Nico knew how Armelle Vilars treasured this garden oasis. He often saw her watering the plants, which were as silent as her patients.

"Hello, Chief. Professor Vilars is expecting you in autopsy."

The receptionist was a new addition. She had two primary functions: greeting visitors and providing support to the families of homicide and accident victims. For years, Vilars had done the job of supporting the families herself, but she had finally gotten the usually callous administration to budget enough money for the receptionist.

"Thanks," he said, nodding to the woman and continuing down the hallway. He felt her eyes on him. Although he didn't pay a great deal of attention to his looks, he knew he had an effect on women. Caroline had once described him as "six feet three inches of muscle, blond hair, and clear blue eyes." He grinned at the memory. As long as he was attractive to her, that was all he cared about.

Inside the locker room, he washed his hands and put on a gown, the ritual required to enter the devil's lair.

"Nico," Vilars said, not even looking up.

He glanced at the stainless-steel table and the coroner's instruments before giving David Kriven a nod. The commander's face spoke volumes, and Nico understood right away. The little girl's body looked like a rag doll. And worse, her organs were piled on a nearby tray.

"We took pictures already," Vilars said. "I'm ready to start the external exam."

Her assistant snipped off a lock of hair and scraped under the girl's fingernails. Vilars swabbed her mouth. Nico listened to the medical examiner as she enumerated her observations. He focused on the words, trying to keep the sight from getting to him.

"The head, thorax, and abdomen all show damage from a sharp object. The assault was brutal."

Nico noted that Vilars wasn't using any personal pronouns. It was *the* head, *the* assault, as if Vilars, too, was trying to contain her emotions. He saw her blink several times.

"The force of the blows dislocated the cervical vertebrae. The eye sockets are empty, and traces of the blade are clearly visible."

Vilars grabbed a thermometer with a flexible probe and stuck it in the girl's ear, forcing it to reach the brain.

Kriven took a step back and looked away.

"The body temperature is unusually low, less than seven degrees Celsius."

After a moment of silence, Vilars looked up, as if to make sure the others understood what she was getting at. "She was frozen."

Her waterproof green smock rustled as she leaned against the table and looked Nico in the eye. "The autopsy is going to be tough and complicated. We're going to have to wait for the body to thaw. I imagine you have better things to do."

"Yep," Kriven said. His forehead had a sheen of perspiration, despite the glacial air-conditioning in the room.

"You'll have my report as soon as possible."

That was their signal to leave. Had Nico been a rookie cop, he might have figured an autopsy couldn't get any worse. But he knew better. He had seen his fair share of worse. He led Kriven out of the room.

"Give me the rundown," he said when they were back outside. He took in the overhead metro line, the honking cars on the street, and the acrid smell of exhaust fumes while he waited for Kriven to collect himself.

"Three students who'd had too much to drink were on their way home from a party," Kriven finally said. "They needed to take a leak and decided to climb over the locked gates at the Square du Temple to piss behind a tree. That's where they found the body. It sobered them right up."

"No surprise there."

"I'm thinking the body got to the park in a suitcase. The team found footprints and the tracks of two small wheels. The rain we had yesterday evening will help us. The ground's still wet. Vidal's getting casts."

"The neighbors see anything?"

"We're canvassing now."

"Keep me posted."

Kriven nodded and hurried to his car. Nico looked at his watch—it was only nine o'clock. He'd swing home to shower and change. His clothes smelled like death.

On the way to his car, images of the girl's mutilated body filled his mind. Who was she? Had she been reported missing? Were her parents searching the streets of Paris for her or waiting by the phone, terrified that their child had been harmed?

Nico shivered. He couldn't dwell on the victim. He needed to focus on the killer. What serious behavioral disorder could cause someone to inflict such violence upon a child? Had a pedophile done this? A twisted father, or a brother, or an uncle? He couldn't bear the thought. Ideas flashed in his mind, one after the other, like a slide projector, each supposition darker than the previous one. For now, he had no way to sift through them all. They piled up in his head until he felt like his brain would explode.

As Commander David Kriven approached the Square du Temple, he could see uniformed officers crisscrossing the green space, their vehicles parked all around.

The park, with its winding paths and colorful flowerbeds, dated back to Georges-Eugène Haussmann's renovation of Paris. A fortress built by the Templars once stood there, and during the French

Revolution, it was the site of a prison where Louis XVI and Louis XVII were held while awaiting their executions.

These days, the Square du Temple, with its English landscaping, ornamental pool and waterfall, ping-pong tables, sandbox, slide, and merry-go-round, drew people from all walks of life, an apt reflection of the culturally diverse and trendy third arrondissement.

That morning, however, yellow crime-scene tape was keeping everyone out. As the police conducted their investigation, residents gawked from their windows and balconies.

"I don't suppose anybody staring down at us saw anything last night," Kriven said, a hint of despair in his voice. "They would have had front-row seats."

"We're still canvassing," Plassard said. "Nothing so far."

"Anything else turn up here?"

"We found tracks on the Rue Perrée side. The team is taking photos."

"He could have parked there and waited till nobody was around to remove the suitcase. He didn't have far to go to reach the fence."

"The park is locked up at night. He climbed over the gate."

"Once inside, it wouldn't have been hard to stay hidden."

Plassard nodded. They started walking toward Vidal and Lieutenant Paco Almeida, who was assisting him. They made quite a pair: Vidal was a grump, while Almeida was a cheerful, optimistic type. Kriven had been paired with Plassard for similar reasons of compatibility—while the captain was laid-back, the commander was a worrier.

"Are you okay?" Plassard asked.

In fact, nothing was okay for Kriven. Although he was still mourning the loss of his newborn—crib death—he was feeling the need to move on. His wife, Clara, however, wasn't ready to do so. She had refused to get counseling, and every attempt he made to renew their intimacy was met with similar resistance. Instead of responding with warmth, she'd search for the pain in his eyes, as though she held his desire to end his grieving against him. He was tired of it. If she didn't want to help herself, he wasn't going to spend the rest of his life that way.

"It's Clara. I think we're done," Kriven said softly.

"I'm sorry to hear that. I know it's been a bitch for a while now. You deserve better."

They reached the tree the students had chosen to pee on, where Vidal was examining the grass.

"Apparently one of the kids had time to pull it out," Plassard said. "Needless to say, it got stuck in his hand."

Vidal chuckled. "He's not going to be urinating in public again anytime soon."

"Got anything?" Kriven asked.

"The body was stiff and cold as ice. The killer didn't bleed her here."

"We searched the park, the playground, and *tutti quanti*," Almeida said.

"Damn, now you're speaking Italian," Vidal said.

"The most notable thing we've got on the weapon is that it's missing."

"So," Vidal said, "our man just came here to get rid of the package."

"In a place we would find it," Kriven said, finishing his thought.

3

As Nico reached the fourth floor of police headquarters, he felt himself catapulted into darkness. One look at Commander Charlotte Maurin, standing as still as a statue, her face stone cold, and he knew what awaited him.

Is language the adequate expression of all realities? Nico instantly recalled Friedrich Nietzsche's question, a remnant from his studies at the elite Paris Institute of Political Studies, a.k.a. Sciences Po. The expression on Maurin's face provided the answer: no. But what other reality lay hidden behind her bleak silence?

"It's bad," she said.

They had gotten another new case during her squad's shift.

"A kid found dead in a middle school. Tenth arrondissement. You coming?"

"Tell me more."

"Kevin Longin, twelve, seventh grade. Had a record for graffiti and fighting. A teacher found him in a classroom at eight this morning. A few kids saw the body before anyone had time to react. I've called in a support unit for them—both the children and the teacher."

"What aren't you telling me?"

"The victim was cut into pieces," she said, almost whispering the words.

"Let's go," Nico said.

Flipping on her strobe and siren, Commander Maurin maneuvered her way into the traffic crawling along the right bank of the Seine. She weaved around the cars as though she were playing a video game full of obstacles. A war game now. They passed the Île de la Cité and Notre Dame Cathedral, then took a left toward the Place de la Bastille.

Sitting beside her, Nico recalled something his direct superior, Michel Cohen, had said more than once: "Humanity is on a slippery slope to hell." Today, he had to agree with him.

Nico focused on the city streets outside the window. They had reached the Quai de Jemappes, which followed the Canal Saint-Martin with its renowned pedestrian bridges and locks. The plane- and chestnut-tree-lined waterway cut through the sea of asphalt and concrete.

Maurin broke the silence. "I can't imagine what the family is going through."

"Don't even try."

"He was just a kid, for God's sake! Like Dimitri. What if something like that happened to your own child? Doesn't the thought haunt you?"

"Oh, I do have my dark moments. And sometimes I prefer insomnia to nightmares. But we have to get over our fears, or else the monsters win. Don't let them stop you and Élodie from having your own children."

Maurin had told Nico that she and her partner were thinking about becoming parents, by either adoption or artificial insemination.

Maurin slowed down as they approached La Grange aux Belles Middle School. A crowd of spectators had gathered in front of the school's bright-blue gates. Uniformed officers were trying—in vain—to keep the cell phones at bay. In a few minutes, images would be circulating on the Internet. These were the times they lived in.

He should never have come back, but the temptation proved too strong to resist. He wanted to understand this stunning violence he had found deep inside himself. It was like an evil genie that had finally escaped from its bottle. He stood in the distance, across from the school, on the promenade that followed the canal. He held a ping-pong paddle and leaned against the public table, looking like he was waiting for his partner to arrive. He had improvised much worse roles before.

He watched the police car turn in to the school courtyard. Seeing how the principal rushed to meet it, he figured this was the top brass. Classy. A tall man in an impeccable suit stepped out on the passenger side. A woman got out on the driver's side. The man was clearly her boss. He had natural authority, a commanding presence. And he was blond. Hot. In other circumstances he would have tried picking him up. Why not? But that was a dream. He was too shy—and too afraid of being judged.

Nothing like the kid had been. There was no condemnation in the gullible little thug's eyes, just candor. Killing the boy was child's play. Intoxicating child's play. Now he would have to wait until the storm had passed—and the magnetic blond man with it—before starting again and feeling the silent calm that followed the flow of blood and the final moan from his innocent prey. It was an elixir running through his veins, keeping his blood young and vital. Forever.

"Chief Sirsky?" In the courtyard, a man held out a limp hand. His features were heavy with stress.

"That's correct. This is Commander Charlotte Maurin."

"Régis Danon, principal. We're beside ourselves over what's happened. The news spread like wildfire, but our teachers have managed to keep our students in their classrooms. Mrs. Hadji is the one who found Kevin. She was unbelievable. She wouldn't let anyone in the room, not even me! She said she didn't want any of the evidence destroyed. I also think she wanted to spare us the horror. She broke down as soon as your colleagues arrived and had to rush to the restroom to throw up."

Régis Danon couldn't stop talking. It was a normal reaction, a need to verbalize the shock and anger. Maurin gestured to Nico that she was heading inside.

"You're trained for this kind of thing," he continued. "We aren't."

Nico nodded. But in reality, nobody could ever have enough training to face a dead child's battered and broken body. And this was the second one in two days. His team stood strong and they didn't shirk their duty—they had no choice.

"You did the right thing," Nico said. "And so did Mrs. Hadji. No one else should have been in that room."

The principal gave him an apologetic smile.

"Have Kevin Longin's parents been informed?" Nico asked.

"Kevin lives with his mother and younger brother. The father abandoned them long ago, which isn't all that unusual for our student body. The majority of our six hundred students come from homes that are disadvantaged in some way or other. It's a challenge for our teachers. But we're in a Priority Education Zone and get supplemental support and training from the Ministry of Education. Kevin is a smart child who could go on to college. His teachers push him to succeed."

The principal paused, realizing, Nico understood, that he was babbling in the present tense. He cleared his throat. "To answer your question, no, we haven't talked with his mother. Your officers said they would tell her." He paused again. "I don't know if it's important, but his grades had fallen in recent weeks. We were getting worried."

"Do you have any idea why?"

"Not yet. I was planning to make an appointment with his mother. Now—"

"Can you show me to the room?" Nico broke in.

They entered the building and climbed the stairs to the second floor, their footsteps echoing in the empty hallway. Nico didn't actually need the principal to find the room since Captain Stéphane Rodon, the crime scene investigator in Maurin's squad, had sealed it off. Nico recognized the local precinct chief, who was standing with two officers in the hallway, just outside the door. They were, in all likelihood, the first officers on the scene. It looked like Rodon was questioning them. Maurin was listening.

Nico turned to the principal. "Mr. Danon, I think your own team needs you."

"Yes, of course," the man said, backing away slowly before turning around and trudging down the hall.

Nico walked over to Maurin, and they stepped away from Rodon and the others to speak privately.

"We're questioning the students and teachers," she said. "The school administration is contacting the parents to come get their kids, and the teachers are organizing a study session for those who can't go home right away."

"And Kevin's mother?"

"Noumen's breaking the news." Captain Ayoub Noumen was the second-in-command in Maurin's squad.

Nico nodded and returned to Rodon, the officers, and the local precinct chief. He noted the man's dilated pupils and dry lips, clear signs of anxiety.

"Thank you for calling us so quickly," Nico said. And he really was grateful. Sometimes precinct cops tried to be heroes.

"Frankly, we don't have what it takes to work a case like this. I hope you catch the bastard."

Nico took a handkerchief out of his jacket pocket, turned the knob, and opened the door.

"I'm done with the door, Chief. Don't worry."

Nico looked over at Rodon. Wisps of his signature red hair were poking out from under the wool hat he often wore. The hat made him less identifiable when he was working undercover.

As Nico entered the room, followed by Maurin and Rodon, the first thing that hit him was the smell of blood. Would he ever get used to it? He looked around and spotted the digital camera on the teacher's desk. Rodon had finished taking pictures, too. It was standard procedure to photograph the entire scene, then take medium-angle shots to establish the relationships between objects, and finally do close-ups of all the evidence. Nico noted the forensic light source, the powerful lamp that filtered light into color bands. It enhanced evidence, picking up details the naked eye couldn't detect, including fingerprints and traces of blood, fibers, and body fluids.

"I haven't come up with much yet," Rodon said. "Just some vague footprints. I'm guessing the murderer put on overshoes. I'm also thinking he wore new gloves."

Sometimes they could get glove prints, like shoe prints, but the gloves had to have some distinguishing marks that came from use.

"Of course, it's a homicide," Rodon continued.

"Slaughter is more like it," Maurin said.

"Yes, it's been a bad couple of days for kids," Rodon said. "Seems like the vampires are after them."

Nico squatted slowly to get a close look at the carnage. Kevin Longin's puffy face was proof enough of the savagery. But his body had also been dismembered, the parts strewn across the room. Nico held back a torrent of curses.

"It looks like he's missing a hand," he finally said after scanning the room.

"Affirmative, Chief. We haven't found his right hand," Rodon said.

"Charlotte, ask the precinct cops to search the school and surrounding area."

"Are you thinking he got rid of it in the neighborhood?" Maurin asked.

"I'm thinking he took it as a trophy, but we don't want to leave anything to chance."

Nico continued to survey the scene. He imagined the killer beating Kevin relentlessly, the teen's suffering giving him unspeakable pleasure, making him feel stronger with every blow. But the boy's death hadn't been enough to satisfy him, so he had proceeded to dismember him.

"There was premeditation," Rodon said. "The guy showed up with a panoply of instruments and left with them. There isn't a single weapon on the scene."

"Sexual abuse?" Maurin asked.

"Probably. The autopsy will confirm that," Rodon answered. He was taking the boy's body temperature to estimate the time of death. "I'd say he died at about ten last night."

"Sunday. Are there any signs of breaking and entering?" Nico asked.

"Apparently not," Maurin said. "We'll double-check, but if not, the killer must have had a key. And he had to be familiar enough with the school to know that nobody else would be here."

Nico nodded. Captain Rodon continued examining the body for clues.

"I'll let you know as soon as I find any hairs," he said. Humans generally lost anywhere from fifty to eighty hairs a day—more than two an hour. And the killer was human—if Nico could call him that.

"The classroom was cleaned Friday night, which works in our favor," Rodon said. "We'll get the cleaning staff's prints, along with those of Mrs. Hadji and the precinct officers, and compare them against any other prints we might pick up."

"Good," Nico said. "Let's figure out how the killer got into the school. When he was finished, he had to get rid of his bloodstained clothes and gloves. Who knows? Maybe he made a mistake, and we'll find something."

"Consider it done," Maurin said.

Nico's phone rang. It was Professor Vilars.

"I finished the autopsy report for the Square du Temple girl and sent it to the public prosecutor. I assume you want me to e-mail you a copy."

Nico thought for a full minute before the medical examiner's breathing brought him back to the present.

"I'll stop by and pick up the report. It's on my way."

"Okay. I'm not going anywhere."

He ended the call and looked at Maurin and Rodon.

"I'm swinging by the morgue. Give this your undivided attention. Maurin, let's touch base this afternoon, okay?"

"Sure."

"If you need help, just say the word. Théron and his squad have been taking it easy lately. I'm sure Rost would love to call them in."

Commander Joël Théron was the leader of another of the division's squads, and Deputy Chief Jean-Marie Rost was one of four section chiefs.

Maurin's shoulders relaxed ever so slightly. Nico had managed to ease some of her stress.

"When you're finished, make sure the crime scene cleaners get here as quickly as possible."

He looked Maurin and Rodon in the eye and nodded.

"Hang in there," he said before closing the door behind him.

"Armelle, you look exhausted," Nico said, taking a seat in the medical examiner's office. "Have you gotten any sleep?"

"I finished the report last night. I knew you needed it right away. Then, since I was already here, I took care of some long-overdue paperwork."

Her hands were shaking as she held out a file folder. The energetic and sharp-tongued medical examiner seemed to be only a shadow of her usual self, which made Nico apprehensive.

He took the report. He quickly scanned the first page, which listed her titles and degrees and specified that the autopsy had been done by order of the public prosecutor with the High Court of Paris. He turned his attention to the specifics: "Name: unknown. Age: approximately 10. Height: 1.49 meters. Weight: 39 kg."

He knew what would come next: a detailed description of the body, the wounds, the organs, the toxicological screening, and the coroner's conclusions. There were several pages of technical details. He looked up.

"Freezing is an excellent way to preserve a body," Vilars said. "It slows biochemical reactions. Therefore, I can't tell you when this child died. I can only confirm that she died from her injuries and not from the cold."

"So she was stabbed to death and then frozen."

"That's right. During the autopsy at eight thirty yesterday morning, her core body temperature was negative seven degrees Celsius. Three hours prior to that, when her body was still in the Square du Temple, Captain Vidal measured negative ten degrees Celsius. Thawing time depends on weight. If the killer used a home freezer set at negative twenty-six degrees, we can establish that she was removed from the source of the cold twelve to thirty-six hours before the first time her temperature was taken. So we can place her murder somewhere between five thirty Friday afternoon and late Saturday afternoon. Since then, decay has followed its normal course, and the bacteria have proliferated with the completion of thawing."

Nico cleared his throat. He didn't need to know all the details. The key piece of information was that the killer's freezer was twelve to thirty-six hours distant from the Square du Temple. Although Nico's investigators could turn that into kilometers, there was no telling whether the killer arrived on foot with his suitcase or waited patiently in his car to dispose of the body at precisely the right moment. Which meant the killer could live right next to the park or several hundred kilometers from the capital—or anywhere in between.

"As you know, the killer removed the victim's eyes," Vilars said. "The two eyeballs found at the Square du Temple belonged to the girl. He also cleaned out her pelvis; certain anatomical parts were neatly excised, while others were ripped out. It's impossible to determine if she was raped. Her vagina was nothing more than a bloody mass of flesh."

Nico didn't know how much more he could take. He stared out the medical examiner's window at the gray waters of the Seine while she continued.

"The knife injuries indicate a standard twenty-centimeter single-bladed knife."

Nico looked back at her. "A kitchen knife, then. The kind you find anywhere."

"Yes. Furthermore, I counted 114 blows to the skull, thorax, and abdomen. Some penetrated the lungs. The liver and spleen were ruptured, and a blow to the stomach caused a hemorrhage in the abdominal cavity."

Vilars stopped talking. Nico waited.

"I can tell you this much, Nico. Based on the angle of knife penetration, I'd say the murderer was right-handed and that the victim tried to defend herself. She had blade marks on her arms and hands, especially on the left side, which would confirm the attacker's laterality."

"Did you find prints or anything else that could be connected to the killer?"

"Absolutely nothing. The killer knew what he was doing and was very careful."

"And truly twisted. He could have covered up the murder. There are so many ways to dispose of a body, but he wanted us to find it. He's looking for a reaction."

Vilars stood up, and Nico took the cue. She had given him all she had.

"Commander Maurin called to say that a middle-school boy is on his way in," Vilars said as she accompanied Nico to the door. "Another homicide."

"Yes, his fate was no better than the girl's."

"How's your team handling it?"

"They're on edge but okay. Call me when you're ready to do the autopsy. The boy's name is Kevin Longin."

"It'll be early afternoon."

Nico said good-bye and returned to his car, where he checked the several messages waiting on his phone. He found a text from his son.

Hi, Dad. Home in an hour. Romain wants to have lunch. I'll call Caroline to see if it's okay. Will take 10 euros from stash.

Nico felt his stomach clench. Dimitri could check in every hour on the hour, and he'd still be worried on a day like this. He stared at the phone before taking a deep breath and turning the key in the ignition.

4

The guard booth in front of police headquarters had been removed. And there were no longer any uniformed officers in front of the large gate that was now double-locked. Nico entered the building like everyone else, through a small door to the left of the gate, which led to a tiny room where two agents did security checks in minimalist conditions. The two agents stood at attention when they saw the head of the Criminal Investigation Division. Nico pulled his smart ID from his pocket and swiped the turnstile scanner. Outsiders were subjected to a walk-through metal detector that was sensitive enough to sound an alarm over the tiniest razor blade, microprocessor, or pair of earrings.

Higher-ups had promised them the latest in both technology and facilities once headquarters moved to the new building in the Batignolles neighborhood. The spanking new seven-story building, with at least two underground floors, would house some fifteen hundred police officers. And 36 Quai des Orfèvres would probably be turned into a museum. Nico felt like a dinosaur—and a little nostalgic. Why? Was he afraid that Commissaire Maigret would no longer whisper in his ear? The celebrated character may have been fictional—invented by Belgian writer Georges Simenon—but he incarnated the spirit of this storied building and served as inspiration for many very real police inspectors.

His steps rang out as he made his way to stairwell A, which led to the Criminal Investigation Division's offices. Nico climbed the worn black linoleum stairs to the fourth floor and headed to the Coquibus room. The space was just big enough for the six members of Kriven's squad but was far too narrow to be comfortable. Only two of the division's twelve squads even had the luxury of working together in one room. The other squads were divided up in adjacent offices. The teams rarely complained, but this was one of the reasons they were moving.

Everyone stood up when Nico entered. He handed Kriven the autopsy report.

"We've heard back from Professor Queneau," Kriven said.

Charles Queneau ran the forensics lab. He would retire in September, and this was one of his last cases. Nico felt sorry for him. A scrupulous and compassionate widower, Queneau didn't deserve such a troubling last case.

"The suitcase was large, with a wheel spread of thirty-four centimeters," Kriven said. "The lab managed to isolate one footprint. It was from a European dress shoe, size 44, with an antislip sole. You can buy this kind of shoe online for twenty euros."

"Our killer is methodical," Nico said. "We can't say conclusively at this point, but I'm betting he's a psychopath rather than a sociopath, as the latter are more inclined to opportunistic criminal behavior."

"That's what I'm thinking," Kriven said. "It could be sexually motivated."

"There's another possibility," Plassard interjected. "Maybe he wants to throw us off and make us think this was done by a sick sex offender when, in fact, it wasn't."

"Anything's possible," Nico said. "Focus on what the Square du Temple residents have to say. We know the killer was right-handed and probably wears a men's size 44 shoe. That's a start."

"Yep, that gives us a very detailed picture," Vidal said, shaking his head.

"Have you checked missing persons?"

France's centralized missing persons office was established in 2002, shortly after a study found that nearly thirty-three thousand missing minors had been reported as runaways. The police realized the urgent need to make a distinction among runaways, kidnappings, and suspicious disappearances and establish procedures to locate the children as quickly as possible. But despite their best efforts, the numbers had actually risen. Of the fifty thousand people reported missing every year, some forty-five thousand were minors.

"They know," Plassard answered.

"We'll send the victim's DNA as soon as the lab gets it done," Vidal said. "Professor Queneau has pushed it to the front of the line."

Not far from headquarters, at the forensics lab, Captain Stéphane Rodon was watching forensic experts inspect Kevin Longin's clothing. This was much more bearable than traipsing through the bloodbath at the school. Professor Queneau had just removed a fiber from one of the boy's pockets with a set of tweezers and was heading over to the polarizing light microscope.

"The fibers are shaped like thin, twisted ribbons," Queneau said, looking through the microscope. "Primarily cellulose, they lack distinctive extinctions and birefringence."

"And in everyday language, that means . . ."

"It's cotton," Queneau replied. "The most common fiber in the world. In fact, white cotton is so common, the fibers are systematically removed from most investigations. But not in this case, because the sample came from the pocket of a kid who was savagely murdered."

"Savagely" was putting it mildly, as far as Rodon was concerned.
"And it's not white," Queneau added.

Captain Ayoub Noumen flopped into a chair, exhibiting none of his usual gallantry. In fact, he was ignoring his partner, Charlotte Maurin, who didn't seem surprised, even though she often chided him for being overprotective.

Nico watched the pair in silence. He knew what had happened. Maurin had made Noumen go to Kevin Longin's autopsy. She'd probably said it would be therapeutic. Ever since being assigned a hit-and-run case and viewing a crushed child's body on one of the morgue's stainless-steel tables, Noumen had used any excuse he could think of to avoid the place. But Maurin had been tough on him today and insisted that he go. Now he was slumped in his chair, his jaw tight, clearly seething with anger. Nico suspected that he was mad at himself—not Maurin—for not doing a better job of managing his emotions.

"Who first?" Nico asked.

Noumen cleared his throat.

"The . . . Kevin . . . Kevin Longin was beaten to death and cut into pieces with a butcher's cleaver by a right-handed man. He was raped post-mortem with a blunt object, something like the handle of a hammer. The estimated time of death is ten o'clock last night. He was murdered in the classroom."

"Kevin's friends said he'd been keeping to himself lately," Maurin said.

"His mother told us he seemed angry, but he wouldn't tell her why he was upset," Noumen said.

"There are no signs of breaking and entering at the school. We think the killer had a key," Maurin said.

"An employee?" Nico asked.

"None of the employees have records. Some of the people we talked to say they saw Kevin with the school handyman several times. According to them, the man has a bit of a drinking problem. He would have keys and access to the classrooms. We're bringing him in."

"The team is visiting cafés and other places in the neighborhood where Kevin might have hung out," Maurin said. "We're also trying to find his father. He took off five years ago. Maybe he had an urge to see his son again."

"To kill him?" Nico asked.

"I know," Maurin said. "It's a long shot."

"He abandoned his kids, which already makes him an asshole," said Noumen, the doting father of three.

"Even if it's highly unlikely, we'll need to question him," Nico said.

Nico's phone rang, and his secretary put Professor Queneau through.

"To what do I owe the honor, Professor?"

"I'm sending the DNA results for the unidentified girl. I hope it helps you find out who she is."

Missing persons had sent over all the names of girls who had disappeared recently. The list was disconcertingly long.

"Let's hope it does."

"Chief Sirsky, I assume Captain Rodon gave you our report on the boy, Kevin Longin. We didn't get much, but I thought that pink-and-red fiber was unusual."

Queneau was suggesting a possible lead. They could ask Kevin's mother if he had some piece of cotton clothing that was pink and red. Maybe the boy had a girlfriend. In all likelihood, it wasn't a serious lead, but criminal investigations never seemed subject to any laws, least of all those of probability.

At the missing persons office in the suburb of Nanterre a few miles outside Paris, the officer was adding the DNA results to the unidentified child's file.

"How long before that thingamajig spits out an answer?" Captain Vidal asked.

The analyst raised an eyebrow. The Criminal Investigation Division was known for its elite, highly educated hires with degrees from the best schools. They were generally more adept at speaking the French language.

"His vocabulary shrinks when he's annoyed," Commander Kriven said.

"I just want to know if someone's pedaling in there or if you've crammed a turbo engine up its ass."

"The problem is, he's easily annoyed," Kriven continued. "He's a good cop, which makes up for a lot. So, is your system a bike or a Bugatti?"

An alert flashed on the screen.

"An SSC Tuatara," the analyst said. "A 1,350-horsepower, 6.9-litre engine that can achieve 276 miles an hour. The fastest car in the world. Sorry about your Bugatti."

The girl's name popped up on the screen.

"Bingo!" Vidal shouted before shaking the analyst's hand. "That machine of yours is a beaut."

Nico sprinted down to the third floor, which was separated from the stairwell by a glass wall. The officer behind the surveillance screens recognized the chief and opened the door, behind which lay the offices belonging to the top brass. Nico turned right, pushed open a dark-red door, and entered a waiting room with polished wood floors and black leather armchairs. The building's skylight illuminated the space.

The deputy police commissioner's office was just off the waiting room. Nico knocked; he got only a growl in return. For some reason, Rod Stewart's raspy cover of "Sunny Side of the Street" came to mind. This was odd, since Nico could never leave his worries at his boss's doorstep—and in his line of work, he was almost always on the shady side of the street. Today was no exception. As he opened the door, the song vanished and an image of little Juliette, the girl from the Square du Temple, flashed across his brain.

Michel Cohen was smoking a cigar at an open window that offered one of the most stunning views in Paris. How many times had Nico admired sunsets over the Seine, the Louvre, and the Pont Neuf from this vantage point, enveloped in a smelly cloud of white cigar smoke?

Cohen turned his attention to two screens that gave him access to the hundreds of cameras throughout the capital that made up the city's video surveillance system. He could pick and choose what he wanted to watch and had a joystick that enabled him to change the angles. Private areas, like apartment windows, were blurred, but the rest of the surveillance system was impressive—and useful for monitoring traffic and demonstrations and for guarding public buildings. *Big Brother,* Nico thought. As useful as the cameras were, he sometimes regretted how society was evolving.

"Damn it!" Cohen grumbled without looking up. "Have a seat."

Nico did as he was instructed.

"So, what do you have?"

"Her name was Juliette Bisot. She was ten years old. Kidnapped four months ago in Louviers, in Normandy. She was walking to dance class, but she never got there. Local detectives quickly concluded that it was a kidnapping. Witnesses saw the girl get into a metallic-gray car, an Audi A3. They even got the license plate, but it turned out to be a fake. Nobody got a clear view of the driver. He simply vanished, taking Juliette with him. Investigators made no progress, even after questioning half the town and tracking down every Audi in the vicinity. And now we know the end of the story. Our only leads are these: the killer used a kitchen knife, is most likely right-handed, wears a size 44 shoe, and has access to a freezer. We think he transported the body in something with wheels, because we found tracks at the Square du Temple."

"The Enfants Rouges neighborhood," Cohen said. "It used to have an orphanage whose children could be identified by their red clothing."

"Red children. What a metaphor."

"Was he caught on camera?"

"The only camera in the area is at the other end of the park and directed toward the third arrondissement's city hall on Rue Eugène Spuller."

"You've got to give me more, Nico. What do the Normandy cops have to say?" Cohen had gotten out of his chair and was pacing.

Nico suppressed a smile. He knew what Cohen was thinking: it was best for all involved to solve the case quickly. The deputy commissioner had taken Nico under his wing years ago, and he had plans for him. He wanted Nico to succeed him one day.

"I contacted the detective in charge of the case," Nico said. "They'd lost all hope of ever finding Juliette. They'll inform the family. The girl's mother is a general practitioner, and her father owns a local business. Juliette was the eldest of two children. I get the sense that the detective was relieved that she wasn't found in their jurisdiction. He'll go see the body at the morgue tomorrow, and I'm sure the girl's parents will make the trip, too. The case file is thick, but has virtually nothing of interest in it."

"So we're starting from zero?"

"I'm afraid so."

"The killer's undoubtedly a sexual deviant," Cohen said. "I'm not buying the theory that it was someone who was settling a score and just wanted us to think he was crazy. Seems far-fetched."

"According to the local police, there's no reason to believe that someone was using the girl to get at the parents."

"But sometimes we don't see what's right under our noses. We both know that, don't we?"

"I'll have the full report shortly, and I'll dive into it right away."

"Whatever his motivation, the bastard planned it down to the last detail. He got fake license plates and found a place to torture the victim and keep her for four months."

The image of Juliette Bisot on the autopsy table flashed again in Nico's mind. An innocent child, beloved by her parents, a good student who was passionate about dancing. She would have become a young woman with her own dreams and disillusions. But Juliette would never know what the future might have held, the joys and tears that would have shaped her life. A man decided otherwise for her.

Cohen shook his head. "If I'd been able to get away with it, I would have had my girls in full-time protective custody."

Both of Cohen's daughters were in their twenties now.

"If only . . ." Nico paused. "But we can't keep our kids locked up till they're adults, can we?"

"No, we can't. And just when I thought my worries were over, now I have grandkids to fret over. So what do we have on the boy's case?"

"We're trying to locate the father, figure out how the killer got into the school, and determine where a fiber found in the boy's pocket came from," Nico said.

Cohen put his cigar out.

"This is going to be a fucking mess."

It was odd how Cohen seemed to be returning to the language of his days on the beat, before he held any positions of responsibility. Was he getting closer to hanging it all up?

"I want you to focus exclusively on these two cases. Now get the hell out of here. We've got two scumbags on the loose. I'm counting on you to nail their hides to the wall, and be quick about it."

Cohen picked up his phone. He had already moved on to something else. Nico heard his boss as he closed the door behind him.

"Call the minister back."

The man was abrupt. But his heart was in the right place.

Caroline wasn't home yet, but Dimitri was. As soon as Nico opened the door, he heard Sting's "Every Breath You Take" blaring from upstairs. The boy's taste in music was spot-on.

But then he stopped in his tracks. Was Dimitri in love? Could that be the reason he was crooning along with Sting? Unless it was a matter of heartbreak, the way Sting felt when he wrote the song. Just yesterday the boy had been dashing around on his tricycle. And now he was into girls. Nico didn't know if he was ready for this.

Nico climbed the stairs. The door to Dimitri's room was open, and his teenaged son was swaying, a fake mike held to his mouth. Nico started singing along.

"Dad!" Dimitri said, lowering the volume. "I didn't know you were home."

"I saw Sting in concert once. Of course, it was after he left the Police."

"I know," Dimitri said, grinning. "You've told me like eight thousand times."

Damn, he was getting old—he was already repeating himself. "Who are you singing for?"

Dimitri blushed. "So, are the cops prying into the private lives of innocent citizens these days? I'm not talking. Even under torture!"

"But I thought you wanted to join the force," Nico said, pretending to be supportive. So far he had managed to avoid telling Dimitri what he really thought. He was hoping to subtly persuade his son to go into a duller, quieter line of work.

"Oh, I still want to go into police work. Just don't try buddying up to me like I'm one of your suspects at HQ. I'm not telling you anything. Sorry."

With that, Dimitri turned up the volume, put the fake mike to his lips, and grinned. *"I'll be watching you."*

Sulking, Nico walked back downstairs. Still thinking about his son, he rummaged through the refrigerator. They had always been close, to the great displeasure of his ex-wife, Sylvie. Dimitri was the spitting image of his father, though he still had some height to gain, and his muscles weren't fully developed yet. They had similar personalities, too. They shared aspirations and even thought the same way. Why, then, this sudden about-face?

He heard the key in the lock, and Caroline walked in. He checked out her curves and lithe legs in her summery dress. But then he noticed the tired and worried look on her face.

"One *salade niçoise* for the lady," he called out.

Her face softened, and her anxiety seemed to dissipate. But why that look on her face? A tough patient? A hopeless case? She was so sexy and so smart. Nico knew he was a lucky man.

She walked over to him and planted a long kiss on his lips.

"How about we go right to bed?" he said.

"You're obsessed!"

"Only with you."

"I hope so!"

She pulled away. There was something off in her tone. "I'll set the table," she said.

Maybe he was wrong, and she was fine.

"Do you know about Dimitri?" he asked.

"Know what?"

"That he's got a girlfriend."

"He told you?"

"He didn't tell you?"

Caroline smiled. "You're pulling an interrogation technique on me. Well, it's not going to work, Inspector! So what did he tell you?"

"Nothing. I guessed. He was crooning 'Every Breath You Take' when I came home, and he blushed when I asked him if he was into a girl."

"To answer your question, yes, Dimitri's in love."

"So he did talk to you about it."

"He asked me for advice."

"Isn't that something dads usually handle?"

"Don't worry. I'm not taking over your job. He's just smart enough to know that if he wants to understand women, it's best to ask a woman. He's like you. He tries to understand."

Nico never worried about Caroline's interactions with Dimitri. She loved the boy as though he were her own. In fact, if Dimitri could have chosen a mother, he might have picked Caroline, because his own mother tended to stress him out.

"If anyone can answer his questions, it's you," Nico said. "As long as this romance doesn't interfere with his schoolwork. He's got to do well on his exams."

"His exams! He's finishing up middle school, Nico, not entering Sciences Po. And Dimitri's a good boy. He's not going to do anything stupid. He respects girls. At some point in the near future you should have that father-son talk with him. But now's not the time."

"I just hope he doesn't hook up with a girl who tries to push him into anything he's not ready for. I want him to take his time and wind up with his own Caroline."

"Don't worry. Your son's smart, and he thinks enough of himself to date the kind of girl he deserves."

"Okay, okay. As always, I trust you. But please keep me posted, and let me know when you think it's time for that talk."

"I think he'll approach you himself. Teenagers can be secretive, but you two are very close. You've got that going for you."

"Yes, Doctor."

Nico walked up behind her and wrapped his arms around her. He kissed her neck and inhaled her perfume. He wanted her. Then he closed his eyes, and instead of surrendering, he shuddered at the vision of the two dead children. He held her tighter.

"Is something wrong?" she asked.

"We've got two cases involving kids."

"I heard about them on the news."

"I can't tell you how grateful I am that Dimitri's older now. If someone tried to abduct him, he could put up a good fight. Still, I can't help worrying, Caroline. I'll always worry."

Caroline was silent for a long moment. "You're right, Nico," she finally said. "No matter how capable and smart your kid is, you can't make the world a safe place to live."

5

Nico was examining the photos of Juliette Bisot and Kevin Longin. Sometimes, with a little distance, the significance of a previously missed detail suddenly became clear.

"You wanted to see me?"

He hadn't heard the knock. He looked up and saw Dominique Kreiss waiting for permission to come in.

"Have a seat," he said, gesturing to a chair. He wanted the opinion of the force's sole criminal psychologist, especially because she specialized in sex crimes.

"I heard on the news about the girl who was kidnapped and held for four months," she said.

"Juliette Bisot's body was frozen until Saturday night, and we'll never know when she died, whether it was right after her kidnapping or much later, unless we get some kind of confession."

Kreiss didn't betray any emotion in her emerald-green eyes. Her work demanded that she understand the criminal mind, and in order to do that, it was better not to feel sorry for the victim. It was a trap that could make a professional vulnerable and less discerning as a result.

"Here are the files for the Bisot case and the second homicide, the Kevin Longin case," Nico said. "They're top priority."

"Was there sexual aggression in either case?"

"Kevin Longin was raped with a blunt instrument, but there was no trace of seminal fluid at the scene or on the body. As for Juliette Bisot, it's impossible to tell."

"Killers in cases such as these tend to be calculating, in control of themselves, and intelligent. They're excited by the idea that the police can't identify them. It intensifies their desire to relive the experience."

"Are you saying that these murderers might strike again?"

"It's very likely."

"Could either homicide be an act of vengeance connected to a family or work-related issue?"

"In those situations, you strangle, drown, shoot in the heart, or poison, but this is about the rape, torture, and amputation of children. It isn't what you usually see with an act of vengeance."

"Maybe one or both murderers are trying to confuse us and send us on a wild goose chase."

"That's possible. But to become a butcher, you need a very serious motive. Sounds unlikely."

Nico didn't respond.

"In any case, I understand the police in Normandy didn't find any revenge connection," Kreiss said.

She knew more about this than she was letting on. Michel Cohen had undoubtedly already spoken to her, aware that they'd need her insight. Nico had nothing to add.

She stood up and headed to the door.

"I'll let you know if something jumps out at me," she concluded, waving the file folders.

It was hot, very hot. Like the man she was questioning, Charlotte Maurin was uncomfortable in this tiny room on the top floor of police headquarters. But the heat served her purposes. The more José Vargas sweated, the better. She could feel his claustrophobia. Maybe she wouldn't have to wait long before he tripped himself up.

"Mr. Vargas, I'll ask you one more time. What was the nature of your relationship with Kevin Longin?"

Her tone was dry, her eyes cold. She knew he didn't like what she was implying—that he was into kids.

"People saw the boy hanging around your office," she said.

"So what? That doesn't mean anything!"

"The school administrators have reprimanded you before, Mr. Vargas. You have a drinking problem. That's not very compatible with your job."

"I learned my lesson!"

"Mr. Vargas, let me remind you that you're talking to a police officer. Were you spending time with Kevin?"

"The kid wouldn't leave me alone. He was like glue."

"What in the world did he see in you?"

"I don't know. He was bored with the other kids."

"So you're a fascinating guy, huh? What was your secret? Did you give him alcohol?"

José Vargas balled his hands into fists. The uniformed officer in the back stepped up to remind the man where he was. His breathing accelerated, and he groaned. Vargas was sweating all over now—from fear and panic. The handyman was about to break.

Captain Ayoub Noumen loved his job. He was proud to be a member of the Criminal Investigation Division, cleaning the scum off the streets of Paris. He liked working for Chief Sirsky and his squad leader. In a word, he was happy. He had no complaints—except at this moment, as he stood in front of Mrs. Longin. How could he hang onto his faith, knowing the evil that had been visited upon her son? Noumen shook his head. He'd never understand. It was in Allah's hands.

The woman's eyes were red and swollen. She was hugging her younger son. Noumen wondered if she'd ever let him go.

"Captain, come in," she finally said, opening the door wider.

The apartment was saturated with the smell of bacon. Noumen could sense it seeping into his clothes. He felt his stomach heave but managed to control it.

"We found a pink-and-red cotton fiber in Kevin's pocket. Would you have any idea where it came from? Could it be from a handkerchief or a piece of clothing?"

Mrs. Longin furrowed her brow. It was hard to read anything but grief in her eyes.

Tuesday was wrapping up when Nico's friend, Judge Alexandre Becker, joined him in his office.

"The prosecutor's put me in charge of Kevin Longin's murder investigation," Becker said. In France, the court—specifically, an examining judge—was always involved in the investigation of a serious crime. Things were moving quickly, proof of the urgency of this case.

The two men weren't surprised to be assigned to the same case. They had worked as a team on many investigations, and the higher-ups liked the results they got. If they couldn't guarantee a conviction in every case, at least they could be sure of a thorough investigation.

"I read the preliminary report," Becker said. "Is the cotton fiber that was found in Kevin Longin's pocket a lead?"

"At this point, we don't know."

"The report suggests that Kevin stole a set of keys to the school and had copies made, which would have allowed him to come and go as he pleased."

"That's correct. The handyman admitted to getting drunk with the boy a couple of times. One morning about a month ago, he couldn't find his keys. He was worried that he'd lose his job, of course. Luckily, when he left home that morning, he found the keys on the ground just outside his door. At the time, he thought they'd just slipped off his belt, and he didn't mention it to anyone."

"I suppose this happened right after he'd been with Kevin."

"Yep. I sent officers to the key shops in the area around his home and the school, but they didn't come up with anything."

"What about the boy's father?"

"We found him. He lives in Marseilles with a woman and their three-year-old daughter. He hasn't left the city in months and hasn't seen his two sons since he walked out on them."

Becker nodded. He knew the type. He had never known his own father, and his mother had raised him on her own, working as a waitress and a prostitute to make ends meet.

"Mrs. Longin told Noumen that he'd stopped hanging out with his friends and was spending time with a new acquaintance," Nico said. "But we have no idea who that person was. We canvassed the entire area and didn't learn a thing."

"Crazy, isn't it."

"We're dealing with a methodical and careful murderer here. Do you know if the Paris prosecutor's trying to get the Bisot case transferred here? Would you be assigned to that investigation as well?"

"It's not in our jurisdiction, Nico. The High Court in Evreux will run that show."

The examining judge from Normandy had already contacted Nico and asked for everything related to the case. The local police had also sent a delegation to the capital. Nico had seen the resignation—even defeat—in their faces. He wasn't surprised. They had spent four months chasing a ghost.

"You met with the parents?" Becker asked.

Nico shivered at the memory. Juliette's parents had gone to the morgue, where Armelle Vilars had spent an hour answering their questions. Then Nico and David Kriven had arrived. If only Mr. Bisot had expressed some anger, or his wife had become hysterical. But that didn't happen. The couple held their heads high, their features frozen in pain. They spoke calmly, almost whispering. But their eyes were what affected Nico the most. They were empty.

"It must have been awful," Becker said.

"It was."

The scene of those broken parents identifying Juliette's remains would be seared in Nico's mind forever, joining the cohort of bloody images that he always carried around. Like Pandora's box, that area of his brain had to be kept sealed off, because when it was opened, all the evils of humanity were set loose in his head.

"Nico?" Becker said. "Where have you gone off to?"

"Back to Greek mythology. Never mind."

The scene replayed in Nico's mind. Armelle Vilars had pulled back the white sheet just enough for the parents to view the girl's face. Her team had done their best to make the child presentable, but no one could remove the vestiges of the devil. Juliette's parents had clenched their teeth and withheld their tears. After a few minutes, the medical examiner had broken the silence: Did they recognize the child?

"They positively identified her," Nico said, trying to shake off the parents' pain. They had been so stoic, dressed as though they were going to a business meeting—Mr. Bisot in a suit and tie and Dr. Bisot in a navy dress with a V-neckline. When she leaned over the body, a necklace with a round medallion swung back and forth like a pendulum, mesmerizing Nico. Had it been another kind of day, he would have asked about it, if only to make pleasant conversation.

Alexandre Becker furrowed his brow. Nico knew what he was thinking. The girl had already been identified via her DNA. Marks such as scars and known medical history, as well as size, race, age, sex, specificities of the skeleton and teeth, fingerprints, and facial reconstruction, could all confirm a person's identity with absolute certitude. A family's visual identification was just a formality. So why inflict it on Juliette Bisot's parents?

"They wanted to see her," Nico said.

"They need to begin mourning."

"Loss requires mourning, and if it is not mourned in full or at all, psychological disorders ensue. Freud, *Mourning and Melancholia*, 1917."

"And seeing their daughter in that state wouldn't lead to a psychological disorder?"

"They insisted. Armelle thought it best to respect their wishes, but she stayed with them, which was the right thing to do. And she didn't show them Juliette's entire body. She knew what she was doing."

They sat in silence for a moment before Nico leaned forward, his expression somber.

"My job is to get into the criminal's mind and try to anticipate where his murderous instincts will lead him next. If I dwell on the child, the image of Dimitri cut up in pieces could settle in my brain, and there's the risk of the father in me taking over. That would be bad for our business, *Monsieur le Juge*."

6

It was decided. The four men in the family—Nico and Dimitri, along with Nico's brother-in-law, Alexis, and his nephew, Bogdan—would take care of everything. It was Ascension Day, a public holiday, and their goal was to install Anya's computer, connect it to the Internet, and create an e-mail address for her. The matriarch of the family was finally taking the plunge. She wanted to communicate with her grandkids, surf the web, and make online purchases. Nico thought she might even join Facebook and open a Twitter account. Ever since the surgeon had implanted a pacemaker under her clavicle, she'd been bubbling with energy.

Anya had recently quoted the Russian prince Alexander Vasiltchikov: "'I shall never forget the calm, almost cheerful expression which flitted across the poet's face as he faced the pistol muzzle already pointed at him.'" He was referring to Mikhail Lermontov, a Russian Romantic poet and dragoon—a military man who traveled by horse but fought on foot and alternated acts of bravery with impertinence before dying in a duel. Anya had felt a figurative bullet skim her own heart, and now a serenity and lightheartedness inhabited her.

Alexis was undergoing his own recovery—an emotional one. He was Anya's physician, and though she had been ill for some time, doctor-patient privilege meant he hadn't been able to tell anyone. To make matters worse, Anya hadn't been following his advice. Nico was furious when Anya suffered her heart attack, but eventually he understood what an awkward position Anya had put his brother-in-law in. Everyone was relieved when she made it through the operation, and the shock of seeing her in intensive care was slowly receding.

Nico was enjoying the sight of his mother bustling about the apartment when he heard his twelve-year-old nephew start arguing with his father about the computer.

"No!" Bogdan grabbed a wire from his father. "That goes here."

Anya put her hands on her hips and scowled at her grandson. "Young man, you shouldn't speak to your father that way."

"Yeah, Bogdan," Alexis said, giving his son a playful jab in the ribs. "Don't talk to me that way."

"I'm just teasing, Dad. But I'm still right."

Alexis put his hands up in surrender. "Okay, I can see when I'm in the company of an expert."

Bogdan did know what he was doing. He loved all technology and had a passion for aeronautics and meteorology. Installing computers was a piece of cake for him.

"So what's next, sir?" Alexis said, tousling his son's hair.

"You mean what's next, *Captain.* That's how you address Boggy," Dimitri said.

"They're all just jealous, aren't they, *tonton,*" Bogdan said, turning to his Uncle Nico for support.

"I have to agree that our future pilot over here seems to know what he's doing," Nico said. "So maybe we should hand the controls over to him."

"Mayday! Mayday!" Dimitri cried out. "We've lost an engine. We need to make an emergency landing!"

"*Aaah* . . . Help!" Alexis said.

"Trays up, and fasten your seat belts!" Nico yelled.

"You boys are a bunch of clowns," Anya said, laughing with them. "Now get my computer hooked up."

The sound of Freddie Mercury's voice interrupted the family reunion, and silence fell like a guillotine. They all recognized Nico's ringtone for police headquarters: "Another One Bites the Dust."

Nico pulled out his phone, keeping his expression relaxed. Although it was a holiday, he had only planned to take a couple of hours off. Two hours too many.

"Chief Sirsky? Commissioner Monthalet would like to speak to you."

The police commissioner's secretary hadn't offered any of her usual pleasantries and didn't wait for a response. Nicole Monthalet picked up immediately.

"A letter addressed to me arrived an hour ago. The security people opened it, because it clearly wasn't from any official source. They informed me of the contents right after they read it. I've already called in Commander Théron's squad to find out who delivered the letter."

That was the commissioner: no emotion and all business.

Nico knew she wouldn't say anything more over the phone. "I'm on my way," he said.

From his mother's home at 112 Boulevard de Courcelles, it would take him about ten minutes to reach police headquarters. He didn't factor in the time he would need to get to his car and climb the stairs to the commissioner's office on the third floor. His siren would make up for the difference.

"Sorry," Nico said, already heading out Anya's door.

"Keep us posted," Dimitri said, turning back to the computer. He had grown up with those urgent calls from headquarters.

Out in the street, Nico glanced at the Alexander Nevsky Cathedral, which Anya attended. He said a silent prayer to the image of Christ above the entrance and then rushed off to headquarters by way of Place de la Madeleine, Place de la Concorde, and the highway along the Seine. Cars pulled over for his siren, and he had to honk at only one recalcitrant driver. He'd heard the urgency in the commissioner's voice. This was no ordinary prank letter. It was something else. But what?

Nico saw the relief on the secretary's face as soon as he walked through the door. She wasn't wearing any makeup or her usual skirt and jacket. She, too, had been called in at the last minute on this holiday.

"Go on in," she said.

Commissioner Nicole Monthalet was at her desk. Unlike her jeans-clad secretary, Monthalet wore a superb beige Burberry trench dress that suited her perfectly and complemented her eye makeup. Without a word, she held out a sheet of paper in a clear-plastic evidence pouch. The message was in red ink, and the slanted handwriting was meticulous.

Nico started reading.

Ladies and Gentlemen at Paris Police Headquarters,
Will you fully appreciate my art? Will you figure out who
I am? Will you stop me in time? Will you stop me at all?
Are you able to? I am your gamemaster.

Mikołaj wszedł przez komin.
Ale gdzie są zabawki?
Schowały się w jego worku.
Oto wychodzą:
jeden mały prosiaczek,
dwa ładny misie . . .

But where is the piglet?

43

"Well, this isn't the first time a head case has challenged the police force," Nico said.

"They don't usually put on such a show."

"Hmm, looks like Polish," Nico said. "But I don't know what it says."

Nico's Russian mother had married into a Polish family that had moved to France generations ago.

"I'll send the original to Professor Queneau. I already called a forensic document examiner," Monthalet said.

"The new guy?"

"Yes, Brice Le Goff. I'll have him send you a copy right away. Find a translator—a real person, I want to make sure we pick up all the nuances. And keep me informed. I'm not going anywhere till we know more."

Nico took the stairs back to his office and picked up his phone.

"Hello?" The man on the other end of the line had the groggy voice of someone who had just been woken up. *He's probably taking advantage of the holiday to sleep in,* Nico thought.

"It's Nico. Sorry to wake you."

"Is something wrong?" Iaroslav Morenko asked in Russian. It was a reflex, as Russian was his native tongue. Under his tutelage, Nico and Dimitri were learning the language of their forebears.

"It's just work," Nico answered in Russian. "Don't worry."

"Criminals don't have any respect for holidays, do they. Then again, we all like to do our favorite things on our days off. How can I help you, Nico?"

"I need someone who can translate Polish."

"Right away?"

"In half an hour, at police headquarters."

Iaroslav whistled. "At headquarters? Cool!"

"You sound like one of the college kids you teach," Nico said. "Do you have someone in mind?"

"I have just the person for you: Małgorzata Włodarczyk. She works with me at the university."

"And you can get this gem of yours here in thirty minutes?"

"Yes, she is a gem, a precious one, and yes, I can have her there right away. She just happens to be right next to me, fast asleep. I'll wake her up and bring her over. I hope it's nothing too gory. She's a bit squeamish. One drop of blood and she'll be screaming for help."

"Just a few sentences to translate. That's all."

"Okay, we'll be there ASAP."

Nico figured it shouldn't take them long to get there. Morenko lived in the thirteenth arrondissement, in "Little Russia," two rows of whitewashed dwellings erected in the early twentieth century above a Citroën garage that had originally been built to house Russian taxi drivers. Nico enjoyed visiting Morenko at this offbeat site near the Butte-aux-Cailles.

Because it was a public holiday, quiet reigned in the maze of courtyards inside the Palais de Justice and the forensics lab at 3 Quai de l'Horloge. Charles Queneau walked down the dilapidated hallway, looking out the ground-floor windows at the temporary modular offices—which had long ago become permanent—and the tables and chairs that the crime scene investigators used on their breaks.

He climbed a flight of stairs to the questioned-documents department, which was responsible for extracting the truth from written words of all kinds. Brice Le Goff was already hard at work, his forehead wrinkled in concentration. That was bad news for the person who wrote the letter. Le Goff looked up when Queneau came in. His left eye was twitching, and Queneau understood what this tic of Le Goff's meant. Something was terribly wrong.

"This red . . ." Le Goff managed to say, his voice tight and barely audible.

"Anything you see or hear in this building is confidential," Nico said, leading them down the hall.

The two professors nodded and followed in silence. Nico knew that being in the legendary Paris police headquarters had that effect on outsiders. He ushered the visitors into his office and handed Małgorzata Włodarczyk the paper.

"Yes, it's Polish."

"What does it say?"

"Hmm . . . it's a counting ditty for kids. Let me see, I can almost make it rhyme in translation: 'Down the chimney comes Santa Claus. But where, oh where, are all the toys? In his big bag, at the bottom . . . *Now here they come: one piglet fair, two teddy* bears . . .'"

Nico jotted down the verse.

"That's a big help. Thank you," he said, standing up and handing her his card.

"If you need anything else, don't hesitate to let me know. Iaroslav is sweet when he says I'm a delicate little thing, but my father was a cop back in Poland, and I heard all sorts of things growing up."

Morenko's jaw dropped, and Nico grinned. This woman was well suited to his Russian friend. He waved down a uniformed officer to accompany them out, his mind consumed by the nursery rhyme.

He reread the letter.

Ladies and Gentlemen at Paris Police Headquarters,
Will you fully appreciate my art? Will you figure out who
I am? Will you stop me in time? Will you stop me at all?
Are you able to? I am the gamemaster.

Down the chimney comes Santa Claus,
But where, oh where, are all the toys?
In his big bag, at the bottom,
One by one, here they come:
One little piglet fair,
Two teddy bears . . .

But where is the piglet?

The author clearly had an exaggerated sense of self-importance: "I am the gamemaster." Why was the poem in Polish? Was it simply intended to throw the police off course? Maybe he just wanted to keep them on their toes, which would support the theory that the man was crazy. Furthermore, the way the letter was written had to mean something. The author had used red ink, and the handwriting itself was formal, as though lifted from the eighteenth or nineteenth century, when writing was an art. Nico shook his head. These were clues, certainly, but hardly enough to establish a reliable psychological profile.

"Can I come in?"

Nico looked up, keeping his cool even though Commander Théron had spooked him.

"Of course."

"You're not going to believe how that damned letter ended up here. At exactly 7:35 this morning, some dude called a courier on Rue de la Tour d'Auvergne in the ninth arrondissement. He told the courier to go to the Square de Montholon, which is close to the courier's agency, where he'd find two envelopes stuck in one of the hats on the Saint Catherine sculpture. One was to be delivered to 36 Quai des Orfèvres. The courier's fee was in the other envelope."

Nico pictured the statue, with its five working-class women linking arms and wearing extravagant hats. Back in the day, unmarried women had donned such headwear on Saint Catherine's Day and gone out in search of husbands.

"The caller said he was a cop pranking his buddies. He used a burner phone that pinged through a tower near the intersection of Rue de Montholon and Rue La Fayette. We're canvassing the neighborhood, but I wouldn't expect much. It's a holiday, and most people were still in bed at that hour."

"Methodical and precise," Nico said. "I'd say we're dealing with someone who has his wits about him—not someone who's just a bit off his rocker."

"I agree."

Cock Robin's "Hunting Down a Killer" played through his head, particularly the line, "But I haven't got a clue." He had the letter, yes, but he was still clueless.

"We need to catch this guy—and fast," Nico said. No way would he let himself feel so powerless.

"The writing is contrived," Brice Le Goff explained. "Any graphic individuality has been blurred. The writing's also diligent. He wanted to make an impression. He pressed down hard, as if he was determined to win or was feeling some intense pleasure."

Professor Queneau took over. "We didn't get any leads from the paper itself. The ink is a fast-drying agent that's perfect for calligraphy. It was made from a nineteenth-century recipe and a pigment used since Roman times—lead tetroxide, which is also called red lead or minium.

It's toxic. Unfortunately, a lot of brands use the same formula. The pen is a classic fountain pen that the author filled by dipping it into an ink-well. He would have needed to refill the pen several times, and he had to be meticulous to avoid having any ink drip onto the page."

"That's it?" Théron asked.

"Not much, I admit. No prints and no specific traces of any kind. But the letters . . ."

Nico shuddered. Tall, heavily slanted letters in red ink. Like blood-ied bodies toppling over.

"I understand why Commissioner Monthalet came in on a public holiday," Queneau said. "This red ink looks like something from a hor-ror movie. Marc and I are going to look into it. We've got an idea. Give us a couple of hours."

"Be quick, Professor," Nico said.

"I understand the urgency. But is there something you haven't told me?"

Nico cleared his throat. "I'm wondering where the little piglet is."

"You're worried that the big bad wolf is about to devour it, right? So am I."

7

It was 7:00 p.m. on the dot when he rang the bell. He liked punctuality—the politeness of kings. Eva opened the door, her face radiant. She was beautiful, with her midlength brown hair falling softly on her bare shoulders. She was wearing a light dress, nothing provocative, but all the more sensual because of it.

"Come in, please."

He held out a small gift. She took it and ripped off the ribbon and paper. He knew how to make the ladies happy. She smiled as she held up the complete works of Oscar Wilde. She kissed his cheek, and he was sure she was pleased with his scent—L'Homme Libre by Yves Saint Laurent. The damsel's final ramparts were collapsing. She was literally falling.

"I reserved a table at Le Moulin de la Galette," he said, his voice deep and languorous.

"I love that place!"

It was a historic restaurant and former windmill in Montmartre, a mythic place that had seen the last of Paris's millers, followed by the *tout-Paris* who frequented the cabarets, and then any number of great painters who immortalized it, including Renoir, Van Gogh, Utrillo, and Dufy. In addition to being romantic, it had a wine list worth the detour. In truth, however, he had never reserved a table.

"Wonderful," he said.

"It's still a bit early. Can I offer you a drink?"

"With pleasure. How is your documentary coming along?" he asked, following her to the kitchen.

She took two flutes from the cupboard and a bottle of Champagne from the refrigerator—a Dom Pérignon worth over a hundred euros. She had means, thanks to Daddy.

"I'll be finished soon, in large part because of your help. You've been a real gold mine of information."

"To the successful completion of your studies," he said, raising a glass to her. "To you . . . and, I hope, to us."

She blushed. For weeks now he'd been warming her up, and she was finally ready. All he had to do was light the fuse and delight in the fireworks of screams and agony. He couldn't wait.

"Another glass?" she suggested.

"That's not what I want," he whispered, gazing into her eyes.

He stepped toward her, wrapped his arms around her, and rubbed his cheek against hers, stoking her desire. He pressed his lips against hers, and a line from *The Picture of Dorian Gray* came to mind: "The only way to get rid of a temptation is to yield to it. Resist it, and your soul grows sick with longing for the things it has forbidden to itself." Oscar Wilde—now there was a master of the genre.

8

Friday, May 10

Nico stared at the piece of paper taped above the bed. The handwriting, in red ink, was the same: "Piglet." An arrow—a monstrous, revolting arrow—pointed to the body.

The apartment was silent, except for the moaning. William Keller—*the* William Keller—was in the throes of grief. Keller was a French Canadian movie director whose work was reminiscent of François Truffaut's and Claude Lelouch's. Critics called it poetic. The public admired him.

Uniformed officers were sitting with him in the living room.

His daughter, Eva, was no longer. The director had dedicated his last project to her. Nico remembered the film, as well as what he had said about the daughter he loved so dearly, the daughter with whom he had shared his passion for filmmaking. She had worked alongside him, working twice as hard as anyone else to earn his respect.

Eva Keller's career ended on Friday, May 10.

Nico's thoughts once again flashed to Dimitri. Eva Keller had been in a safe field of study. But what about Dimitri, bent on pursuing an occupation that could conceivably put his life on the line every day? Yes, he was proud of Dimitri, but in the face of this father's grief, he didn't know if he could bear the anxiety.

Eva Keller was twenty-one. She was studying at the French film school La Fémis, a highly selective institution with an international reputation and an impressive list of graduates, including William Keller himself.

"Let's get started," Nico finally said.

The squad's crime scene investigator picked up her digital camera and started shooting the scene. When she finished, she began methodically diagramming the room. Even seemingly unimportant details could ultimately be a lead.

Commander Joël Théron opened the drawers of the armoire and felt around for clues. Nico, however, couldn't take his eyes off Eva Keller. The weapon—a screwdriver—had been left behind on the bloody sheets.

Lisa Drill, the crime scene investigator on Théron's team, was now leaning over a shag rug and vacuuming up dust and particles, which would be examined later.

"Not much point in housecleaning when you're just going to mess it up again," Théron said, pointing at the black fingerprint powder, fiber duster, and lifting tape.

Drill shrugged. On other cases she might have had a comeback to lighten the mood, but not now. It was just too grisly. She finished collecting the trace evidence, glanced at the body, and looked at Théron, her face expressionless.

"Commander Théron always acts like a jerk when he's freaked out," Nico said.

Drill nearly smiled.

"He's right," Théron admitted. "My wife never laughs at my jokes. She calls them predictable, like all men."

"Not all men," Dominique Kreiss said, nodding at the sight on the bed. She walked over to Nico, who filled her in.

"Eva Keller, twenty-one, a film student at La Fémis. Her mother tried to call her last night and again this morning. She got worried, because they always talk before Eva goes to class. When she didn't hear from her by noon, she asked Eva's father—the film director, William Keller—to drive over to her apartment to check on her. He found her like this. He managed to call it in before collapsing in the hallway."

"There's no sign of a break-in," Théron said. "Either he was invited in or he rang the doorbell and pushed his way in."

"The killer has a clear penchant for cruelty," Kreiss said as she stared at Eva's body. "He's someone who gets his pleasure from making his victim suffer. Only someone who's extremely sadistic could inflict these injuries."

"Sadism and masochism are sometimes closely connected," Nico said.

"Yes, Sigmund Freud coined the term sadomasochism. According to him, a person could be both sadistic and masochistic and derive extraordinary sexual pleasure from either dominating or submitting. That's why sadistic killers often prefer weapons such as knives, which allow them to get close to their victims. You may not believe this, but a sadist capable of doing what we see here could also have suicidal urges."

"Are you telling us that he might be acting out a death wish?" Théron asked.

"It's possible. He could be acting on some morbid fantasy that he's carried around for some time."

"How do you explain the fact that after beating and mutilating this woman, the killer took the time to brush her hair?" Nico asked. "Look at that ponytail. It's perfect."

"Indeed, that is strange," Kreiss said. "In any case, the killer had a taste for the aesthetic . . ."

A crime scene tech had just put bags over the victim's hands and feet to preserve trace evidence. He was preparing to do the same with her head.

"Wait," Nico said.

He carefully turned Eva Keller's head, revealing a massive blow and a ribbon around the ponytail.

"Get that to the lab immediately," he told the tech. "It's urgent."

Théron shot him a questioning look.

"Pink-and-red cotton, like the fiber found in Kevin Longin's pocket."

Nico could feel the room getting several degrees chillier.

"Finish up here. I'm going to go talk to the father."

Two officers were bringing in the body bag. Nico gave them a nod and headed down the hall to the living room. William Keller was sitting on the couch, his face swollen and his eyes red from weeping. Images of his eviscerated daughter would haunt him to his dying breath.

"I'm Nico Sirsky, chief of police with the Criminal Investigation Division."

As he extended his hand, Nico spotted the vomit stain on Keller's shirt. Now he could smell it, too.

"She was all I had." His voice was toneless.

Nico remembered seeing a newspaper photo of the father and daughter at the Cannes Film Festival. Keller had his arm around Eva, and the look on his face was one of absolute devotion.

"I have nothing left . . ."

"Does your wife know?"

"We still live together, but we've led separate lives for some time now. Our marriage will never withstand this." Tears rolled down his cheeks. "To answer your question, no, I haven't told her yet. She still thinks I'm looking for Eva."

Keller covered his face and moaned like a mortally wounded animal.

Nico waited.

Finally, the father looked up, pleading with his eyes. "You'll tell her, right?"

Nico asked Théron to send a team to the Keller home in the nearby suburb of Saint-Germain-en-Laye.

"Was your daughter seeing anyone? Did she have a boyfriend?"

"She wasn't very interested in boys her age. She thought they were immature. She had flings, but they never lasted long. She wasn't ready to settle down."

"To your knowledge, had she been having one of those flings lately?"

Keller shrugged.

"Did Eva confide in her mother?"

"Not much, as far as I know. She and I were closer."

"And how were things at school?"

"Her professors had nothing but praise for her work. She was going to be a great director—the best in her generation!"

"Had she received any threats?"

"Not that I know of."

"Have you gotten any threats?"

"Me? Never!" The director looked away, his jaw clenched.

"What is it?"

"The star in my last movie."

"The one who got the César Award for Best Actress?"

"Yes. She's married to a director and has two children. She doesn't deserve to have her life ruined. She's a good woman. A dear friend."

"Did you have an altercation with her husband?"

"Just an argument. You can't be thinking . . . Even an angry husband wouldn't do such a thing!"

Keller started sobbing again.

"I'll have someone take you home."

"Where?"

"Home, to be with your wife."

"For so many years, I've only felt at home in two places: on the set and with my daughter. She was my inspiration. I made my films for her, and her alone. Do you have children, Chief? Being a parent is complicated. She was so smart, so pretty and full of life. She gave her all to everything she did. I have no reason to go on . . ."

Nico was worried that Keller might hurt himself. He'd advise Mrs. Keller to get some help for her husband.

"Inspector, you'll catch him, right? You'll get the monster who killed my child."

"I'll do everything in my power. I give you my word."

"The bastard has to die. From this day on, it's my *raison d'être*."

William Keller stood up, and, for the first time, Nico got a good look at him. The director was tall and actually rather handsome. He could pass for a movie star himself.

"I'll keep you informed, Mr. Keller."

William Keller turned and walked out of the apartment without looking back. Nico shook his head. For the first time in his life, the man who had directed hundreds of actors and actresses had no script to follow.

"We finished with the room," Théron announced behind him. "The body's on its way to the morgue. We're about to start going through the rest of the apartment."

"Will Professor Villars be doing the autopsy?"

"She's waiting for us."

"Perfect. I have to go back and give Commissioner Monthalet an update."

"We're already canvassing the neighbors. I've sent Eva Keller's cell phone to the lab, and I've got a detective contacting her school."

"We need her timeline. Be quick about it. I don't want the killer getting too far ahead of us. And one more thing: William Keller was having an affair with a married woman, a well-known actress. Let's check out the husband."

"You got it, Chief."

That the slain woman was the daughter of a celebrity would surely raise the profile of this case. The homicide would be all over the news, and the last thing his division needed was to be caught in a media feeding frenzy.

Nico left the building, where Eva Keller had lived in a loft with a magnificent rooftop deck and ivy growing over the white walls. He walked through a small courtyard. Closing the wrought-iron gate behind him, he stepped onto the Place Jean-Baptiste Clément. He was just around the corner from the Sacré-Coeur Basilica in Montmartre, a neighborhood filled with poetic cobblestone streets and secret passages, dotted with villas, intimate cafés, and vine-covered hills.

Nico suddenly recalled Lucie Valore, the widow of painter Maurice Utrillo, who had proclaimed herself Empress of Montmartre and proposed to Salvador Dalí that he become its emperor. Nico was a fan of the surrealist painter's work and knew that he had lived not far from here.

Nico occasionally swapped his morning jog for a walk through Montmartre—but only before 10:00 a.m. After that, the streets were overrun with tourists. The neighborhood would be teeming with crowds today. The police cars had already drawn onlookers and promised to attract many more once news got out that the famous movie director's daughter had been slain.

He was walking to his car when his cell phone rang. It was Caroline.

"Nico, have you heard from Dimitri?"

"No, why?"

"I got home early from the hospital today, and it doesn't look like he's been here. He always leaves a note if he's going out."

Nico double-checked his texts. Nothing from Dimitri. That wasn't like him. He always checked in.

"I have no idea where he is," Nico said. His heart began to race. "Please make some calls. Maybe he went to Anya's after school, or Tanya's."

"Right away, sweetheart."

Nico could hear the tension in Caroline's voice. They ended the call, and Nico hurried to his car, trying to quell his rising anxiety.

A ten-year-old girl murdered in Normandy. A boy butchered in a middle-school classroom. And a young woman slain in her own apartment.

He needed to find his son.

9

Sensing her presence, Nico looked up from his desk. Caroline stood in the doorway, looking as beautiful as ever.

"Hi. I need to talk with you about a couple of things before you come home," she said. "Nico, I don't want you to be too hard on Dimitri."

Caroline had located the boy. He'd been studying with his new love at a café. She had called Nico immediately and told him that his son was safe and sound.

"Dimitri and I are going to have a long talk," Nico said. "I don't know what's the matter with him. He's getting downright airheaded."

"That's what I mean. I don't want you to come down on him. He was just studying with his girlfriend and forgot to leave a note. He assured me that it won't happen again. And you—overreacting's understandable, considering what you've got on your hands."

Nico walked over to her and put his arms around her waist. He felt the tension drain from his shoulders. She had a way of calming him, and he needed to clear his mind, if only for a few minutes.

"I wish I could get away," he said, nuzzling her neck. "What are your plans?"

"I'm taking Dimitri out to dinner. Sylvie was supposed to, but she called and said she couldn't make it."

"I'm not surprised. She's always letting him down. Where are you going?"

"Higuma, on Rue Sainte-Anne."

It was a traditional Japanese restaurant that served big bowls of noodle soup, fried dumplings, and sautéed meats. Nico loved the bustling place. The chefs, shaking huge woks behind the counter, prepared dishes in record time.

"Are you sure you can't come?" she whispered.

"No, I can't," Nico said. "We have another homicide: William Keller's daughter."

Nico felt a tremor run through Caroline.

"Is something the matter?" he asked, pulling away and looking at her face. She was biting her lip.

"What could be worse than losing a child?" she said softly.

"You're right. I worry so much about Dimitri. God knows what I'd do if I had more than one kid."

They stood together in silence for a moment.

"You said you had a couple of things on your mind?"

"Oh, it's nothing, really," Caroline said, avoiding his gaze. "We can talk about it later."

He pulled her close again. "Thank you for taking care of Dimitri. He's lucky to have you."

"I'm not his mother."

Now Nico was confused. Caroline had taken Dimitri under her wing, as if she had known the boy his whole life. And he considered her his second mom.

"You know how much you mean to him."

"Yes, Nico, I do. I should go now. He's waiting for me."

Nico tried to hold on to her, but she stepped back.

"The car's in a no-parking zone. I've got to go."

Nico stood in the middle of his office and watched her leave without so much as a good-bye. What had he done? Caroline disappeared, leaving her enchanting perfume behind.

A minute later, Deputy Chief Rost walked in, with Commander Théron on his heels. "We've got a lead."

"The ribbon?"

"No, no results on that yet. It's about the letter."

Nico took a deep breath and focused his attention on them.

"Queneau and Le Goff have an intriguing theory."

Heading toward the forensics lab, the three men made their way through the interior courtyards of the Palais de Justice, only to find themselves blocked by a locked gate. A drop-off was taking place on the other side—prisoners scheduled to appear before a judge were being transferred to holding cells.

Nico shook the gate.

"Inmate arrival in progress," a uniformed officer called out.

"It's Chief Sirsky. How long? We're in a hurry."

"Hello, Chief. How many are you?"

"Three total."

"I'll open up for you."

Nico and his colleagues hurried past the ground-floor cells to the lab entrance. They climbed the steps two at a time to join Queneau and Le Goff, who were waiting for them. They led Nico, Théron, and Rost over to a computer right away.

"This is the letter sent to police headquarters," Queneau said.

Le Goff moved the mouse. "Here's another letter that looks like it came from the same person."

"Shit, no!" cried Théron.

The handwriting and ink color were identical. And the other letter was also in Polish.

Le Goff translated, "'There is no happiness without tears, no life without death. Beware, I'm going to make you cry.'"

"What does it mean?" Rost asked. "Who wrote that?"

"The Red Spider," Le Goff responded. "The taunting tone, the long, spindly characters in red ink, the sarcastic humor. It's a textbook case."

"Can you be a bit more specific?" Nico asked.

"Lucian Staniak, a.k.a. the Red Spider, a nickname derived from the red ink he used to write to police and the media," Professor Queneau explained. "According to urban legend, he was a Polish serial killer who committed at least twenty homicides from 1964 to 1967, primarily targeting teenage women. His homicides were sadosexual in nature and included mutilation, a bit like the Whitechapel Murderer."

"You mean Jack the Ripper?" Nico asked.

"That's right. Eighty years after the infamous Englishman went on his killing spree, Lucian Staniak launched his own. Other similarities with our current killer are that he murdered on public holidays and used a screwdriver."

Lucian Staniak, Jack the Ripper, and now this guy. It was the stuff of horror movies. Except that this was real and far scarier. *If only this were a movie,* Nico thought. Better yet, if only he could snap his fingers and find himself next to Caroline and Dimitri at Higuma. Caroline . . . He'd have to figure out what was up with her.

"What happened to Lucian Staniak?" Rost asked.

"He was arrested on January 31, 1967, and sentenced to life in a psychiatric hospital," Queneau said.

"The writing looks exactly the same, but it can't be him," Théron said.

"Indeed, it can't," Le Goff said. "However, the writer tried hard to imitate it. I would add that he's skilled. This is the work of an artist."

"'Will you fully appreciate my art? Will you figure out who I am?' Those were his words," Nico said.

"He's playing a game of copycat," Queneau said.

"This is no game," Nico said. "Excellent work, men. Now we need to figure out what it means."

Back at headquarters, Nico passed Commander Kriven's desk. He was wolfing down a sandwich. Eva Keller's murder and the Kevin Longin investigation didn't make the Juliette Bisot case any less urgent, even if another jurisdiction was involved. Nico knew that Kriven would eat all his meals from the vending machines if he had to.

Nico wanted to find out more about this Red Spider. He had attended a European Police College conference organized to encourage cooperation among law-enforcement agencies in different countries a few months before, where he had met a cop from Europol who could probably put him in touch with a Polish liaison officer. As soon as he was back at his desk, Nico called the Europol headquarters at the Hague.

"Roselinde Angermann. How can I help you?" The woman at the other end sounded German, but she spoke in English.

"Nico Sirsky here."

"Nico! How are you?" she asked, switching to French.

Angermann spoke four or five languages—Germans tended to be good at that. She had teased him about his monolingualism when she met him, but joked that the French kissed better than the Germans.

"I'm great, thanks. Are you still running?" he asked.

"I'm training for the New York City Marathon."

"I'm impressed. So, have you met your soul mate yet?"

Angermann's career had always been her priority. But over drinks one night during the conference, she had confided that she feared she would never find Mr. Right. She had taken heart when Nico told her that he was very much in love. She thought it might not be too late for her.

"I'm seeing someone, but it's too soon to tell," she answered. "Tall, dark, good-looking, Mediterranean. To what do I owe this call?"

"Are you familiar with the movie director William Keller?"

"Of course. I love his movies. Has something happened to him?"

"His daughter, Eva Keller, was murdered."

"How can I help you?"

"We could have a copycat on our hands."

"Who do you think your killer is imitating?"

"Lucian Staniak, a Polish serial killer from the 1960s."

"You want details from the locals. Is that it?"

"That would help, yes."

"I'll get on it right away, and I'll call you as soon as I have something."

With that, Roselinde Angermann hung up.

10

Saturday, May 11

Nico tiptoed across the room. He felt his chest constrict as he took one last look at Caroline, breathing softly as she slept, before closing the door behind him. He had wanted to make love the previous night, but for the first time since they had been together, she had claimed she wasn't in the mood. Had he done something? He was too afraid to ask. He just kissed her on the cheek before she turned away.

If only he could wait for Caroline to wake up, he would be able to see whether everything was fine. But he didn't have a choice. There'd be no weekends off for him as long as there were three murders to solve. Although he insisted that his detectives get their family time, he didn't live by his own rule.

He drove to headquarters in a funk. As soon as he got in, he called Deputy Chief Rost.

"I'm reviewing the SALVAC questions now," Rost said.

Commissioner Nicole Monthalet had fought hard for a violent-crime database similar to that of the FBI's Violent Criminal

Apprehension Program. Both systems were designed to detect serial crimes by comparing and linking unsolved cases. Nico had ordered Rost and Dominique Kreiss to fill out the one hundred questions on the search form, and they had spent the better part of the night on it.

Nico listened as his deputy chief continued. "Professor Queneau just shared his conclusions regarding the ribbon found in Eva Keller's hair. I'll be right there."

When Rost arrived, he held out a number of enlarged photos and read from the report. "'The two samples are 100 percent cotton. The chemical composition and dyes are identical. Furthermore, the fibrils have the same axial inclination. Without a doubt, the fiber found in Kevin Longin's pocket matches the ribbon removed from Eva Keller's hair.'"

Nico took the report and looked through it.

"Your intuition was right," Rost said.

The two men looked at each other in silence, taking in the full significance of this discovery.

Nico finally spoke. "You know what I think? The killer planted the fiber on the boy, knowing that he would use the same material to tie the hair of his next victim. He's planned out every one of his moves, and he's testing us."

"There were no prints on the message we found on the wall in Eva Keller's room or on the screwdriver. In fact, we found no trace evidence at all in the apartment. Nothing. That's rare. This killer is very skilled."

"Skilled? Let's not give him that much credit. What about the blood in the room?"

"The splatters on the walls and sheets match the splatters a screwdriver would make. The one we found is being tested for DNA."

Nico's cell phone buzzed. He didn't recognize the number.

"It's Małgorzata Włodarczyk. Do you remember me?"

"Of course. Would you hold for a moment, please?"

He put the phone down and turned to Rost. "Launch the SALVAC search, and ask Dominique to work on the killer's profile."

Rost nodded and left, and Nico picked up the phone. "What can I do for you?"

"It's about the letter I translated for you. I told you that it's from a children's counting song. 'Down the chimney comes Santa Claus. But where, oh where, are the toys? In his big bag, at the bottom . . . One by one here they come: one piglet fair, two teddy bears . . .'"

Nico listened to her humming the tune.

"I thought you might like to know the rest of the lyrics. 'Three round balloons in tow, four planes a pretty lemon yellow, and five yummy candies—oh!'"

He almost laughed. He didn't know what to make of it.

"Thank you," he said. "That could help."

"I told you. My father was a cop—in Gdansk."

Poland: a country that had once even disappeared from the map of Europe, partitioned among Russia, Prussia, and Austria. Today, it was a member of the European Union.

"I learned from my father that even the smallest detail could lead to something in an investigation."

Her accent, which emphasized the penultimate syllable in each word, was charming.

"I'm crossing my fingers for you, Chief. Don't hesitate to call if you need me."

Nico thanked her again and hung up, wondering what the song could mean.

Nico and Alexandre Becker met for lunch at Ma Salle à Manger, a restaurant in the Place Dauphine known for its hospitable atmosphere and southwestern French cooking.

Florence, the energetic owner, greeted them like old friends and guided them inside, away from the crowded outdoor tables. Posters of

Bayonne and red-and-white checked tablecloths made them feel like they were in the Basque country. Braided heads of garlic and peppers decorated the room.

"Here's a quiet table where you can discuss your business. Don't worry about that table of ten over there. It's reserved for a group of Brits, and they won't understand a word you say. How about a pitcher of Gaillac, a special vintage I keep for my favorite customers?"

"Sorry, I'm on duty," Nico answered.

"Now, now, Chief. Working on a weekend? You've got to relax a little, or else you won't be any good at work."

"Whatever you recommend," Becker said.

Florence winked and headed back to the counter to slice up a fresh baguette on a vintage guillotine cutting board. She grinned as she placed a bread basket and a bottle of red wine on the table a couple of minutes later.

"And how are your lovely ladies?" she asked.

At that moment, the English diners, animated and clearly eager to eat, walked into the restaurant. Nico gave Florence a thumbs-up to indicate that all was well in their personal lives, and she hurried over to welcome the group.

After seating the newcomers, Florence instructed the server to take Nico's and Becker's orders: *cassolettes de lentilles* to start, followed by a *tartare de canard aux endives* and *piquillos à la luzienne*. In a flash, the woman trotted down the stairs to the kitchen.

"That's a lot to be eating in the middle of the day, Nico," Becker said. "We'll be falling asleep at our desks."

"No chance of that happening. I can't remember the last time I ate."

"What a mess," Becker said. "Three horrific murders, one of them a celebrity's daughter, some devilish letter written in red ink, and the only clues so far: a fiber, a ribbon, and an apparent link to a fabled serial killer."

Nico was keenly aware that an investigating magistrate would have a hard time holding on to a semblance of independent thinking against a media onslaught, public opinion, and pressure from the higher-ups.

In situations like this, even those with the best intentions could wind up trying to save their own skin.

"I suppose you know by now that the prosecutor has tossed me the hot potato," Becker said.

Their server returned with their starters.

"What's the story with Lucian Staniak? It sounds ridiculous. I can see the headlines already: 'The Red Spider's New Web.' Next thing we know, Marvel will come out with a graphic novel based on a character by the same name."

"According to Dominique Kreiss, we've got a psychopath on our hands. He's methodical, intelligent, and clever. He chose his victims with a precise pattern in mind."

"Logically, that kind of murderer preys on a specific type of victim. Jack the Ripper killed prostitutes from poverty-stricken Whitechapel. All of them were older, with the exception of the last one, who was only twenty-five. The crime scenes were similar, and he killed them all in the same manner."

"I'm aware of that. But there's a big difference between Kevin Longin and Eva Keller."

Florence interrupted the men as they were sopping up the remnants of the *cassolettes* with their bread.

"Don't your lady loves make you anything to eat?" Florence said, refilling Nico's water glass.

"How could anyone rival your cooking?" Becker asked.

Florence grinned. "You're making me blush. I'll get your main course."

Becker turned back to Nico. "I want to talk to you about the second message."

"'Piglet.'"

"That raises the question: Who are the two teddy bears?"

"Kevin Longin," Nico said.

"And the second?"

"I've got a bad feeling about this. You know how coincidences make me nervous. You don't think that—"

Nico's phone buzzed, and he reached for it quicker than he'd meant to. He caught Becker's questioning eyes.

"Is something wrong?"

"I was hoping it was Caroline. But no, it's from Europol."

"You look disappointed."

Alexandre Becker was a friend. In fact he was like a brother to him.

"I don't know. She seems a little distant these days."

"With you? You've got to be joking. That's impossible."

"And yet . . ." Nico could barely say it.

"You must be imagining things. Maybe something is going on at the hospital. Do you want me to have a word with Stéphanie? She and Caroline are close."

"No, Alexandre. I'll figure it out. We should eat and get back to the office."

Nico opened the e-mail from Europol, printed out the report, and dived in with Becker.

Staniak lived to make his victims suffer. He'd cut them open, eviscerate them, and lay out their intestines, kidneys, and reproductive organs for show. Unlike Jack the Ripper, he liked his victims young. He was sexually frustrated and had no moral compass.

Nico interrupted the silence. "Can you believe that Staniak wound up living out his life in an asylum? After he got the death sentence, they decided he was too crazy to execute."

Becker sighed, setting the report down on Nico's desk. "In many countries—France included—a killer has to be of sound mind to be sentenced to death. When someone is *non compos mentis*, society doesn't have the right to execute him. In Staniak's case, it seems his parents and sister had died in a car accident caused by a female driver who was never prosecuted, and Staniak murdered young women who looked like her."

"Yes, but Staniak's homicides weren't just revenge killings. He had a thirst to be recognized, a drive for power and domination, and sexual perversions as well."

"Staniak had a mental illness nobody could heal. He was *non compos mentis.*"

Becker got up and walked over to the window, and Nico returned to the report.

"Do you think that's the case with our killer?" Nico asked, fearing he already knew the answer.

He didn't wait for a response. He continued reading about Lucian Staniak. And then he noticed something. A shiver ran up his spine. Eva Keller hadn't been chosen at random. It was time to call everyone together.

"I'm listening," Deputy Commissioner Cohen said as he strode through the door and took a seat. Cohen was a short man, but he always made his presence known.

"Commander Théron, start with the autopsy," Nico said.

"The assailant struck the victim in the back of the head, knocking her out. Then he cut open her belly with the screwdriver found at the scene, pulled out her organs, and spread them over her body."

"What was used to knock her unconscious?" Becker asked.

"A blunt object that has yet to be found," Deputy Chief Rost said.

"Wait a second," Nico interrupted, looking through his files. "Lucian Staniak used a bottle of vodka to knock out his last victim. Furthermore, she was eighteen and a student at the Kraków film school. Eva Keller was a film student. What if that's why the killer chose her? Maybe he was copying the Red Spider down to the last detail."

"Okay, but why Eva Keller?" Becker asked. "The school has other students."

"Perhaps our copycat wanted to take it up a notch," Dominique Kreiss said. "Killing Eva was bound to get a lot of media attention."

Everyone fell silent for a moment.

"She was murdered around midnight," Théron finally said. "And the man who did it was probably right-handed. Unfortunately, the autopsy yielded no other new clues."

"What about the girl's school?" Cohen asked. He was sitting on the edge of his chair, fingering a cigar.

Théron answered, "The school's president didn't have anything especially significant to say. Eva was extremely talented, which we already know, and had a promising future ahead of her, thanks in part to her famous father. That said, she wasn't conceited, and she got along well with her peers. Both the teachers and the other students liked her. Nothing unusual seemed to have occurred recently. I have a list of staff and students. We'll be calling them one by one."

"What about William Keller's affair?" Nico was tapping a pen on his desk.

"I contacted the actress," Rost answered. "I promised to keep the affair quiet, as long as it had no bearing on the homicide. And I do believe it's unrelated. We have an appointment tomorrow morning— with you, Chief." He looked over at Nico.

Théron whistled, and Nico gave him a half smile. He was just trying to lighten the funeral-parlor atmosphere.

"Being chief has its perks," Nico said. "Has the lab pulled anything from Eva Keller's phone?"

"We're comparing her four hundred or so contacts with the students and staff at her school. She was very organized. Practically all her contacts were grouped according to how she knew them. One number caught our attention: it belongs to a certain person named Wilde. They talked on the phone quite a few times on the day she died. The number hasn't shown up on her phone since Thursday."

"It's clear that Eva Keller had a date with Wilde at seven on Thursday," Rost said. "It's in her calendar, but no location is indicated."

"A boyfriend?" Becker wondered.

"It's too soon to tell," Théron said. "And the neighbors have nothing to say, other than that she was pleasant, quiet, and polite. Like the rest of Montmartre, the square she lives on is always full of people. That said, it was a public holiday, so the streets were less busy than usual."

Cohen finally spoke. Nico felt the man's dark eyes bore through him as he verbalized the urgency of the situation: "We need to find this guy before he kills another Eva Keller—or Kevin Longin."

Nico turned to Dominique Kreiss. "Do you have anything more on the killer's profile?"

"He's throwing me off, I have to admit. I base my profiles on the way a serial killer murders, mutilates, and disposes of bodies, on the places the homicides are committed, and on the characteristics shared by the victims. This information allows me to draw up a portrait. Here, on one hand, we have a copycat. Eva Keller's murderer imitated Lucian Staniak. On the other hand, he also took out his aggressions on a teenage boy, who is a very different kind of prey. And the location is very different as well."

"His MO is different, too," Maurin said. "With Kevin Longin, he took a trophy—the hand. If he's copying someone, and it's not Staniak, who is it?"

"It's all very curious," Kreiss said. "I'm missing something . . ."

"*We're* missing something," Nico corrected. "What if there are two of them, working together, but each with their own method?"

"At this point, anything is possible," Cohen said.

"Some psychiatrists say that copycats don't copy exactly," Kreiss said. "Each killer is unique. Some get close, though, like Heriberto Seda, who was sentenced to life in prison in 1998 for murders in New York. He copied the Zodiac Killer, who was never caught. That said, even a copycat would have his own signature."

Cohen stood up, signaling that the meeting had come to an end. "You've got your work cut out for you. Nico, I'm counting on you."

Everyone filed out of the office, except Alexandre Becker, who walked over to his friend. "This seems to be getting to you, Nico."

"It is. I feel like I'm just waiting for another homicide. Will it be a child? A woman? A man? I don't know where this guy is headed. I can't figure him out."

The magistrate put a hand on Nico's shoulder. "You have the singular ability to slip into the minds of the worst criminals. It's one of the things that makes you a great cop. You'll find him. And remember, we're still in the early phases of our investigation."

"Yep . . ."

"And don't worry. This thing with Caroline will work itself out."

Nico frowned and waved Becker away.

"Call me if you need anything. I'm available twenty-four seven— you know that."

Nico gave him a friendly slap on the shoulder, and Alexandre Becker left the office. Back at his desk, Nico turned his attention to the little girl's homicide. No sooner had he opened the file than he realized what was bothering him. A tiny detail. A mouse that could bring an elephant to its knees.

He picked up the phone and entered the number. A woman answered. He'd have to sound reassuring. He knew how to do that— how to fake it if he needed to.

"Good evening, ma'am. This is Nico Sirsky, head of the Criminal Investigation Division in Paris. We met a few—"

"I remember."

Nico picked up on the tension in her voice. The police had called incessantly over the past four months, never bearing good news. She had no reason to expect differently now. Her daughter was gone. But the dread would always be there.

"I'm sorry to bother you. I have just one question."

"I'm listening."

"When you declared your daughter missing, you gave the police a description of how she was dressed."

"That's correct."

"I see that Juliette was wearing a ribbon in her hair."

"She wanted a ponytail that day."

"What did the ribbon look like?"

"It had little pink-and-red flowers." Nico heard a sob on the other end of the line.

"Ma'am. I'm going to e-mail you a photo. Please take a look at it, and let me know if it could be Juliette's ribbon."

"Have you found Juliette's killer?" Nico could hear another sob coming, and he steeled himself.

"Not yet, Dr. Bisot. I promise we'll let you know right away if we have something new to report."

"I'll check my e-mail."

"I'll call you back in five minutes."

Nico sent the photo of the ribbon and waited. He watched the second hand swoop around the face of his wall clock. Around and around. He suddenly thought of Dimitri and Joni Mitchell's song, "The Circle Game." His son was growing up and turning into a young man, one who was concerned about others. He would likely make a good cop.

The phone rang. "Dr. Bisot!" his secretary called out.

"Put her through."

"It's the ribbon Juliette was wearing."

Nico quickly thanked the grieving mother and hung up. He headed out the door. Professor Queneau would be in the forensics lab. He was sure of it.

"Can you check for traces of Juliette Bisot's DNA on the ribbon found in Eva Keller's hair?" he asked as soon as he walked into the lab.

"I'll get on it right away."

11

Sunday morning. Suit and tie. Breakfast at Ladurée, a hub of Left Bank chic at the corner of Rue Jacob and Rue Bonaparte in Saint-Germain-des-Prés. Nico and Deputy Chief Rost were seated at a round wrought-iron table on the veranda. Rost had chosen the cushioned love seat, and Nico a leather lawn chair next to a palm tree. It would have been difficult to get any cozier or more elegant. Guests melted into the sur-roundings, having left the stresses of the outside world behind them. But for Nico, it was another day at work, and even at Ladurée, the colorful macarons did little to distract from three bloody murders that needed to be solved.

Several customers gave the award-winning actress a once-over when she made her appearance. Did the real-life person live up to their impression of her? Nico surmised that the ones who ignored her were tourists who hadn't seen any of her films.

The two men stood up to greet Marianne Delvaux. She sat down at their table and removed her dark glasses. William Keller had good taste. An impeccably dressed waiter took their order for hot drinks, fruit juice, and a basket of minicroissants. They wasted no time bringing up the matter of her relationship with the director and his daughter, Eva.

"I can't imagine the horror of losing a child," she said.

Nico picked up a tremor in her voice. Was this the mother talking or the actress? In any case, her presentation was spot on.

"I agree," Nico said. "Did you know Eva?"

"Of course. I saw her several times. She was very talented."

"Did she know about your relationship with her father?" Rost asked.

"I don't think so."

"You don't *think* so?"

"Eva had a sixth sense, that's for sure. And she had an uncanny ability to pick up on little details. I don't know if it was because she was always behind a camera, or if her eye for detail is what drew her to filmmaking. No matter. I can't be certain that she didn't understand what was going on between William and me."

"Did she ever seem annoyed or angry with you?"

"Absolutely not. She was always polite, and she idolized her father. She'd never embarrass him."

"So she wouldn't care that he was betraying her mother?" Rost pressed.

"William and his wife weren't on the best terms. And to tell you the truth, I wasn't William's first affair. He has always loved women. He's a collector."

"That doesn't seem to bother you," Nico said.

Marianne Delvaux laughed. "Don't be such a prude!"

She bit into a little *pain au chocolat*, showing off her sparkly white teeth. She was certainly sure of herself.

"What about the argument between William Keller and your husband?" Nico asked.

"Oh, that . . ."

"Your husband must have been terribly angry with William Keller to seek him out like that."

"He was posturing. He wanted William to back off. To tell the truth, I had no intention of breaking up my marriage. William is pleasant enough and good company, but I had no desire to start a whole new life with him. His charm was wearing off."

The actress's words struck a chord. Was Caroline growing tired of him? He was always getting called away. His life was full of violent crime. And it seemed that he was leaning on her more heavily than ever to look after Dimitri. What had she said? "I'm not his mother"? He'd been so selfish! After all, she had a career of her own—a career that was just as important as his. He'd make it up to Caroline—do whatever he needed to do to fix things. Nico made a mental note to call Tanya. She always had good advice.

"Does your husband ever get violent?" Nico asked.

"If you're imagining that he could have done something to Eva, you're mistaken. He's working in Los Angeles."

Nico knew that. The team had already checked. Her husband had a solid alibi, but pushing her could possibly bring to light some lead.

"You have a son, is that correct?"

"That's right. He's a student. I keep him out of the limelight, and he's doing well. Don't involve him in this, please."

"Have you heard of anyone called Wilde?" Nico asked.

"Oscar Wilde?"

"A boy Eva was seeing."

"No, that doesn't ring any bells."

"Did she have a boyfriend?" Rost asked.

"You, sirs, are trying to pull one over on me," the actress said, smiling coyly. "You just suggested that she had a boyfriend named Wilde."

The woman was clever.

"Let me put it another way," Rost said. "Did you ever see Eva with a boyfriend?"

"And let me be clear. William and I didn't involve our children in our relationship or discuss them. If I saw Eva, it was by chance, or it had something to do with my work. William and I were having a casual affair—nothing more. Sometimes you need a breather from a long-term relationship. Sharing your day-to-day problems can kill any sense of passion."

Nico felt a knot in his stomach. He put his croissant down.

"In any case, I don't know anyone who had anything against Eva. Nothing that could lead to murder, to commit such a barbaric act."

They were wasting their time. Nico paid the bill, and he and Rost returned to headquarters.

Commissioner Monthalet gave Nico an odd look, as if by the power of her mind alone she could rip the key to the enigma from his brain. But he didn't have it yet. He was just putting the pieces together.

"Professor Queneau is sure: the DNA on the ribbon belongs to Juliette Bisot."

"Three murders. A serial killer," the commissioner said.

Robert Ressler, a former FBI agent and author, had coined the term "serial killer." In the 1970s, Ressler had conducted interviews with nearly forty serial killers in an effort to profile violent offenders and find parallels between their motives and backgrounds. Nico was familiar with his work.

"Juliette Bisot and Kevin Longin are the 'two teddy bears,'" Monthalet said. "He executed his victims in cold blood. But I'm wondering if there was some trigger, something destructive enough to transform him from a merely troubled person to a murderer."

"For Lucian Staniak, it was the car accident that robbed him of his loved ones," Nico said. "But for the person we're chasing, it could be anything: a breakup, job loss, humiliation, frustration, or a number of other events that would cause internal conflict. The killer might be responding to a lack of recognition or an act of aggression, and killing is his way of assuming control again. When he murders, he's no longer under the thumb of a person or fate itself."

"What's your next step, Chief?"

"Kriven and his team will take the lead. I want to get our top computer researchers on this, too, and see what they can dig up."

"What are you thinking?"

"Radically different MOs, no single signature that applies to all three homicides. I'm thinking he's mimicking more than one serial killer."

The commissioner leaned back and smoothed her impeccably designed jacket. "Prove it."

She had thrown down the gauntlet.

"I'm on it, Commissioner."

"In the meantime, I'll deal with the top prosecutor. We've got a hundred and twenty magistrates, and I want to make sure all these investigations are under one person."

That person would undoubtedly be Judge Becker.

"Keep Deputy Commissioner Cohen and me in the loop. We're available whenever you need us."

Nico wanted to go home to see Caroline and his son, but he couldn't leave just yet. Still, he needed a break.

He grabbed a special key and unlocked a door that opened to a narrow staircase with a low ceiling. The stairs didn't lead to some hidden wonderland, but instead to the air-conditioned evidence room. Nico walked across the tiny space, his footsteps loud on the cold tile floor. He went up the five wooden steps at the back of the room and opened the French windows. And there it was—the rooftop. He climbed out and perched on the zinc and slate tiles. The view was breathtaking. This was where he always came when the going got tough.

Many of his fellow citizens seemed to believe whatever they read on the Internet—no questions asked. They thought that serial killers were an American thing. But one of the earliest serial killers was a marshal in the French army, Gilles de Rais, who fought alongside Joan of Arc. He raped and murdered at least a hundred and forty children in the Vendée region. He was tried as a witch, and after being sentenced to death, he was hanged from a gibbet above a raging pyre. France had others: Joseph Vacher, the Jack the Ripper of the Southeast; Henri-Désiré Landru; and the French doctor Marcel Petiot.

The rest of Europe had its fair share of infamous murderers as well. One of the most notorious was Elizabeth Báthory, nicknamed the Blood Countess and Countess Dracula. The countess was accused of killing hundreds of young women in Hungary. She beat, burned, and muti-lated her victims, sometimes biting the flesh off their faces before freez-ing and starving them to death. It is said that she bathed in their blood afterward, convinced that it would preserve her youth. The idea that serial killings were rooted in some sort of moral decline or American imperialism was just hogwash.

Enough, Nico thought. The three homicides were beginning to consume him. The walls he had built between his personal life and his work were tumbling down, and he felt vulnerable. He pulled out his cell phone. His hand shook as he entered his sister's name.

"Nico?"

He shivered.

"Nico, what's going on?" Tanya asked gently.

"It's Caroline," he said in a near whisper.

12

Nico was at his desk and ready to get underway before dawn. He intended to turn his office into combat headquarters.

"We're looking for a serial killer whose crimes are modeled on famous predecessors, a man who's trying to prove that he's as good as or better than the masters," he told his colleagues as soon as they were gathered together, coffee cups in hand. "His letter challenges us to stop him."

"We need to find out which killers he copied in the Juliette Bisot and Kevin Longin homicides," Alexandre Becker said.

"Rost, I'm going to put you in touch with Roselinde Angermann at Europol," Nico said. "Send her the case files, and see if any of our European colleagues respond. Helen, can you get in touch with the FBI? Meanwhile, Bastien, comb the Internet and your various networks."

Helen Vasnier and Bastien Gamby were the division's go-to Internet researchers.

"Maurin and Kriven, I want your teams looking everywhere else. Théron, you and your team can continue to investigate Eva Keller's homicide. Put a face on Wilde. Let's go!"

On Sunday evening, both France 24 and CNN had aired pieces on William Keller and the death of his brilliant daughter, who had been following in his footsteps. The media spotlight was on Nico's Criminal Investigation Division, and the glare was bound to get harsher. As soon as the reporters found out that the killer had two other notches on his belt, the crimes would go viral. Meanwhile, the killer was savoring his notoriety. Of this, Nico was sure.

The night before, as Nico had turned off the television, Dimitri had looked at him, his eyes shining with pride. "Caroline told me you were working on the Keller case."

"That's right."

"Any suspects yet?"

"The case is more complex than it appears."

"I'm sure you'll get the guy, Dad."

Nico had smiled.

"I'd help you out, but I don't have my badge yet."

"Ah . . . Get yourself through high school first, kid."

"Details, details."

The bantering had continued until Nico realized that Caroline wasn't joining in. She was fussing around the kitchen, indifferent to the world around her, walled up in her thoughts. She had come home late from the hospital, blaming a problematic case. But Nico's gut was telling him something else. His ulcer was aching again. Was she seeing someone? Could he survive if he lost her?

The regional police archives' nine kilometers of shelving were overflowing with dusty files of violent, bloody tales. Charlotte Maurin, David

Kriven, and two of their team members were meeting with a couple of administrative officers. The pair was an odd mix of computer geek and library rat, a rare, dual-personality species.

Kriven handed over the list of cases, and the administrative officers started pulling out books, dissertations, notes, and reports.

"The whole notion of a copycat killer is a media creation," one of them said.

"What do you mean?" Kriven asked.

"Nobody kills for the sole pleasure of imitating a famous serial killer," the second one explained. "Maybe a killer gets his inspiration from a serial killer, but the drive to murder—if it's not an act of passion—is rooted in the killer's personality. Often it's the result of childhood trauma, either physical or emotional."

Kriven gave this some credence. According to one US study, almost 40 percent of convicted serial killers had been physically abused as children, half had suffered psychological abuse, and almost a third had been sexually abused. Of course, the great majority of people who had suffered terrible abuse as children never committed any serious crimes as adults.

The first administrative officer set down a pile of books. "Killers express their fantasies through unique signature rituals. In any case, dismemberment often reveals a fragmented mind and the nature of the violence the killer experienced as a child. You'll find that in the textbooks."

"If there's any chance at all that a list of our killer's idols will shed a ray of light on his personality and provide us with a lead, we must seize it," Maurin said. "There have to be scores of serial killers who've left their own mark. We need to review them all."

Kriven was pacing. He loved his job, but some parts of it he could do without. "As if we didn't have anything else to do with our time! We'd better get some coffee."

◆ ◆ ◆

Helen Vasnier was at her computer, chatting away cheerfully with an FBI agent in perfect English.

"Good-bye, John, and thanks for your help."

Deputy Chief Rost, who had just ended his call with Roselinde Angermann, looked over at his colleague. Either the FBI agent was a man willing to go above and beyond—it was painfully early in Washington—or Vasnier had her ways.

"So it's 'John' now, eh?" Rost asked.

"He's such a gentleman," Vasnier said, giving him an enigmatic Miss Marple smile. "He's running our cases through their database."

"And?"

"Nothing yet. What about you?"

"I like that Angermann woman. I think she takes sadistic pleasure in disturbing her colleagues' peace and quiet. And she's like a pit bull. Once she's got her teeth into something, she won't let go."

"Well, I hope so. We might not get much from the FBI this time."

"Why's that?"

"Call it intuition. How much are you willing to bet?"

Rost declined. He never bet against Helen Vasnier.

The Internet was overflowing with serial-killer fans and serial-killer fan clubs. When it came to books, movies, and television series, the members could go on and on. They talked about their favorite killers, argued over memorabilia going up for auction, and expressed their fascination with the various victims. Bastien Gamby thought they were all crazy. But they knew what they were talking about.

Gamby challenged them to guess who the serial killer was based on a description of the crime scene. A while later, he spotted the message: "IK."

"How do you like that?" he mumbled. "'I know.'"

A name came up, followed by the details.

"Well, shit," Gamby said loud enough for everyone else to hear.

Rost's cell phone vibrated in his pocket.

"Europol has something," Roselinde Angermann said when he answered.

Before he could respond, his land line rang. "Can you hold on?" he asked. "I have another call."

It was Commander Kriven. "We've got something."

"Andrei Romanovich Chikatilo, the Butcher of Rostov," Gamby said, back from his online foray and once again among the living.

"I know who he was—one of the worst serial killers the Soviet Union has ever known," Kriven said. "It would be safe to say one of the worst criminals ever." He nodded in Nico's direction. "He was Ukrainian, like you. It hasn't exactly been wine and roses over there."

"Okay, David. I know all about Ukraine—and Russia," Nico said. "Gamby, tell me about this guy."

"Andrei Chikatilo was a teacher and a father of two. It's believed that he committed more than fifty murders—boys, girls, and women—between 1978 and 1990, primarily in Rostov-on-Don. He mutilated his victims with a knife, cutting them up and ripping out their organs. He also gouged out their eyes—that was his signature. He probably couldn't stand his victims looking at him. He was finally arrested and sentenced to death, then executed in 1994 at the age of fifty-seven."

Maurin added, "One of his victims, Olga, was a ten-year-old girl. He lured her from the bus with him and took her to a cornfield. Once there, he stabbed her more than fifty times and removed her bowels and uterus. Her body was found four months later in the snowy field. The cold had preserved it."

Just like Juliette Bisot, Nico thought.

Kriven cleared his throat. "For Kevin Longin, the criminal inspiration was Thomas Quick, whose birth name was Sture Ragnar Bergwall. After a robbery conviction he was confined to an institution for the insane, and while he was undergoing recovered-memory therapy, he confessed to thirty-three homicides between 1964 and 1993. On the basis of his confession he was found guilty of eight murders. Later, however, he retracted his statements. He'd been given a high dosage of benzodiazepines during therapy, and while heavily drugged he'd simply invented the confessions. The convictions were thrown out for lack of hard evidence. Ultimately, he was released from the hospital, and the whole episode became a legal scandal in Sweden."

"Kriven, I'm waiting," Nico said. "Get to the point."

"According to his stories he played sexual games with the bodies of the boys he killed. He dismembered them and took parts of their bodies as trophies."

Nico stuck a pin in a map he had hung on the wall. Judge Becker walked over to look at it. Red pins denoted where the original serial killers had carried out their crimes: Ukraine, Sweden, and Poland. Green corresponded with the places where the bodies were found in Paris: Square du Temple in the third arrondissement for Juliette Bisot; La Grange aux Belles Middle School in the tenth arrondissement for Kevin Longin; and Place Jean-Baptiste Clément in Montmartre for Eva Keller.

"Any thoughts?" Becker asked.

"Sometimes there's logic behind a killer's movements," Dominique Kreiss said.

"Who else will he copy?" Becker asked. "Who'll be his next victim?"

"The FBI came up with nothing," Vasnier said. "Apparently he hasn't done anything over there."

"It looks like he's touring Europe—a serial killer's Europe," Nico said. "If that's the case, we can probably assume that he's not hearing voices that tell him to kill. He's too rational. Most likely, he's a psychopath who fits in, for all intents and purposes, which makes him all the more dangerous."

"Even a rational killer surrenders to his weaknesses," Becker said. "Consider Kemper's necrophilia."

"You're right. But does his pleasure come from committing the murders or from perfectly imitating his predecessors?"

"Ms. Kreiss, what do you think? If I understand correctly, profilers don't readily accept the idea of a copycat," Becker said.

"That's correct. In fact, we don't have many studies on the subject. Most psychiatrists and profilers believe that every serial killer has a signature. Each one has a ritual that corresponds with a particular fantasy, even when the killer's imitating someone else. In any case, our killer needed a trigger. Serial killers are very sensitive to failure, which they experience as the worst kind of humiliation, and they tend to have big egos. Of course, they have no empathy for their victims and no capacity for imagining the suffering they inflict."

"So why haven't we figured out our guy's signature?" Becker asked.

The room fell silent. Finally, Kriven spoke up. "We have the ribbon in Eva Keller's hair. It's allowed us to link the murders."

"And there's the content of the letters," Théron said. "It's not the same as what the Red Spider wrote. The killer sent us a personal message."

Becker nodded. "The counting song. What about the victims?"

"Our victims seem to resemble past victims and their circumstances," Maurin replied. "Juliette Bisot, for example, was kidnapped on her way to dance class. Chikatilo abducted a girl who was taking the bus to her piano lesson. Eva Keller was a film student and was knocked unconscious before being murdered. Lucian Staniak's last victim was attending film school in Krakow and was knocked out with a bottle of vodka. As for Kevin Longin, he was similar to the young boys Thomas Quick was accused of murdering."

"So where does that leave us?" Frustration was written all over Becker's face.

"Nowhere," Nico admitted. "We've got prints from the wheels of a suitcase and a size 44 shoe from Square du Temple. Witnesses spotted a five-door Audi A3 where the girl disappeared in Normandy. In the Longin case, we're still looking for the person the boy was hanging out with. Similarly, we're trying to identify the Wilde with whom Eva Keller had a date on the evening she was murdered. And finally, we know the killer was right-handed. Dominique, I understand you have a theory regarding Wilde. Is that correct?"

"Oscar Wilde, the well-known nineteenth-century Irish writer, was an elegant speaker with a fine mind. He had a reputation for provocation and paradox. His comedies were a hit during the Victorian era. But he had a liaison with the wrong woman's son—homosexuality wasn't socially acceptable at the time—and was subsequently tried and convicted on charges of indecency. He was sentenced to hard labor in prison. After his release, Wilde was impoverished, but he continued writing and even experienced a spiritual awakening. I'm thinking that Eva Keller's enigmatic date didn't choose the name by chance, and that he's the murderer. He reproduces crimes like great forgers replicate the works of the masters. And in doing so, our killer's trying to shake our sense of morality."

"On that score, we haven't had any luck," Rost said. "Eva and the killer talked several times on the phone, but he was using a burner."

"And nobody at her film school knows who this Wilde guy is?" Becker asked.

"It seems not."

"What about her contacts?"

"I've had people on it for hours," Théron said. "We haven't found a thing."

"And in the SALVAC?"

"No trace of our copycat," Nico said.

"Rosie said the same thing," Rost said.

"Rosie?" Kriven asked, and everyone's face relaxed a bit.

"Roselinde Angermann, from Europol."

Nico pressed on. "Send out notices to the local precincts. I want them to inform us of any homicides with no clear suspects."

"So, is it going to take a fourth victim for us to get anywhere in this investigation?" Becker was shifting in his chair, and Nico could see that he was getting agitated.

"The killer is looking for prey similar to his idols' victims, which means he will likely carefully select his next victim. Louviers is more than a hundred kilometers from Paris. We need to research how and why the killer was in Normandy. We need to keep looking for leads."

"Ladies and gentlemen, we're chasing one of the worst killers the capital has ever known," Becker said, getting up from his chair. "Jack the Ripper lacked creativity by comparison."

13

He stayed close to the buildings, brushing past the residents of Paris rushing from one obligation to the next and the tourists who were just as focused—bent on seeing the city they had dreamed of visiting before they died. For his part, he was cool and calm. He had reached a higher state of being. He was exactly where he wanted to be and knew that it was only a matter of time before his genius was recognized.

He approached the commercial hub of the Left Bank, a hive of activity. According to the guidebooks, the cafés, restaurants, and cinemas in this neighborhood bore witness to the area's creative and bohemian past. What a rip-off! What remained from the time when Modigliani, Picasso, Matisse, and Chagall roamed the Boulevard du Montparnasse? When Apollinaire, Sartre, and Cocteau rubbed shoulders with Hemingway, Faulkner, and Fitzgerald on the Rue de la Gaîté? The towering Tour Montparnasse built in the early 1970s had swept away any remnants of that golden age. But he had returned to honor the memory of those greats; he was their heir.

Heir to Fritz, with his round face and solid body. A debonair-looking man. But what did he like most about Fritz? His white hands with their long, graceful fingers perfectly adapted to sewing and making pastries. Fritz would have preferred to have been born a woman, wearing pretty dresses and making dolls, but that wasn't in the cards. So he had rented a shop with living quarters in the old city of Hanover during the Weimar Republic, after the bloody defeat of the German Empire had thrown the country into upheaval and caused rampant inflation. The chaos was a godsend for Fritz, and the flourishing black market was a perfect venue for his small-time trafficking.

The Paris Montparnasse train station rose before him, just as the central railway station, with its statue of Ernest Augustus, King of Hanover, had once risen before Fritz. In Paris, more than a hundred and seventy-five thousand people used this station every day. And like other train stations around the world, it attracted the marginalized of society: bums, good-for-nothings, street vendors, pickpockets, and prostitutes, many of whom were often drunk or high. All of their stories were sad and lacking in originality. Having been beaten and/or raped, they had fled their homes and fallen prey to drug use and soliciting. He had no compassion for these human larvae.

For several weeks now, he had been hanging out here, watching the nighttime fauna of this underworld. He had found him sitting on a bench—a little too pale, a little too skinny, with bags under his eyes. He was around twenty. He would do. He would let himself be picked up by a lecher, taking a few bills for a blow job in the bathroom. The boy would have pleased Fritz.

How would Fritz have approached him? He envisioned him in a suit and tie, looking serious, asking to see the vagrant's papers. He was an informant for the Hanover police and often passed himself off as a cop. Clever. He saw Fritz approaching the boy and watching the little color in his cheeks drain away, dreading that he'd be arrested and thrown into a cell stinking with piss.

"Ain't got no papers," the kid would have said. "But I'm a good boy . . ."

"A good boy. If you say so . . ."

"I swear it, sir."

The boy would have looked at Fritz with puppy-dog eyes.

"Listen, I don't like seeing you begging like this. Come with me. I'll give you something to eat. Maybe I can find you a job."

"A job?" The boy's eyes would have shone.

"That's right, son."

"I'm ready to work hard, sir!"

"You'll have to be nice . . . *very* nice."

Hearing these words, the boy would have hesitated—just a bit. But a second later, he would have looked up and nodded. If he didn't grab this opportunity, somebody else would. This kind of luck never came twice. He needed a protector. Why not this guy?

"I'll do whatever you say," he would have said.

Fritz would have smiled and taken the boy far from the station.

Now it was time to apply Fritz's methodology. The homeless boy followed without putting up any resistance. If he had to be *nice* in order to eat, sleep under a roof, and have a job, it was worth it. But this fallen boy didn't know how much more would be asked of him. He was about to take a one-way trip into hell.

They walked a long way, from one boulevard to another, until they reached the Seine, near the Eiffel Tower. For Fritz, it would have been the Leine River, lined with half-timber houses and red-brick buildings.

He had rented a furnished three-room apartment in a residential hotel. It offered a superb view of Paris. The kitchen had a stove, a refrigerator, a microwave, a dishwasher, and a coffee machine—everything he needed for 240 euros a night. It also had a fitness room and an indoor pool, but he had no interest in those amenities.

In the elevator, the homeless boy watched the floors rush by and nearly leaped with pleasure, like a kid in an amusement park. Despite his hard life, he was surprisingly naïve. Once in the suite, he stood at the window, his mouth hanging open. The Seine snaked at his feet. The boy had clearly spent far more time underground than in high-rises.

He lit a candle and lowered the lights. Then he pulled out some canapés and chocolates and poured two glasses of Champagne. The boy watched, stupefied.

"To a new life!" he said, raising his glass.

The boy's hand trembled as he followed suit, gulping the Moët & Chandon. It could have been cheap bubbly. His palate wouldn't have known the difference.

The boy's stomach rumbled.

"Go on," his host said, pushing the plate of canapés toward him. "Eat."

The boy's eyes held a mix of incredulity, gratitude, and joy. He had long ago lost his final remnants of dignity. Solitude, poverty, and drugs had stripped him of his humanity. He was ready to become a slave in exchange for food and lodging.

"The bathroom is over there. Take a shower. Use plenty of shampoo and soap. You stink."

The boy rushed to do as he was told. The man listened to the water run, got undressed, and lay down on the bed, his head propped on a pillow and his organ erect, much to his surprise.

While the boy was showering, the man thought about Fritz. He had used his own modest home, but the neighbors had sometimes complained about the strange sounds. They probably wondered about the boys who came home with Fritz but never left. They quickly forgot when he provided them with baskets full of food. He always had plenty of black-market pork. Quiet stomachs calmed rumors, and nobody ever asked where he got the meat.

The boy returned, smelling clean. Finally, it was time to get down to business.

14

It was ten in the morning when Kriven entered Nico's office. He was frowning.

"We've got something on Eva Keller. She was working on a documentary with two classmates. They said it was supposed to be a simple project, but Eva had turned it into a real piece of investigative journalism. Guess what it was about."

"I give up. What?"

"Serial killers in the movies."

Nico put down his pen and studied Kriven closely.

The commander was a ball of tension. He had something other than the investigation on his mind. Nico waited for him to spill it.

"I need to tell you something, before you hear it from anyone else," Kriven finally said. "Clara and I have decided to separate."

Nico cringed. He had been hoping that Kriven and his wife would make it. He couldn't help seeing his own life in their failure. First a divorce from Sylvie, and now Caroline was becoming more distant with each sunrise. Before going to work today, he had tried to take her in his arms, but she had stiffened and pushed him away. And the look in her eyes. Was it sadness? He had faced challenges head-on his whole life. But this morning he had just walked out.

"I'm sorry," he told Kriven.

Kriven gave him a weak smile. At a loss for words, Nico was grateful when Maurin stuck her head through the door. "We've got a report from the twelfth arrondissement. Something odd in the Bois de Vincennes."

The Bois de Vincennes on the eastern edge of Paris was the largest public park in the city.

"What kind of odd something?" Nico asked, his eyes still on Kriven. Although he'd appeared dour just a minute earlier, Kriven had clearly shifted into high gear.

"A leg."

The Bois de Vincennes, spread over nearly ten square kilometers, had wooded areas, gardens, a zoo, a farm, several theaters, a castle, a Buddhist temple, and a velodrome. Larger than Manhattan's Central Park, it was a paradise for local families and athletes. It was also a refuge for the homeless, who set up tents wherever they could, and a place where prostitutes worked from vans parked along the roads. The park had seen more than a few grisly murders over the years.

Local precinct officers in black jackets had taped off the scene. Members of the canine unit, meanwhile, were holding back their impatient and noisy dogs. Nico greeted the officers and introduced his teams. Both Kriven and Maurin had brought their full squads.

"Okay. What do we have?"

"A fisherman discovered a severed leg half immersed in the water here," the lead officer said. "He didn't touch it. He was too afraid. We'd seen your memo about reporting any crazy-ass crimes."

"Crazy-ass" wasn't in the memo, but the officer's interpretation was spot-on.

"So we called you."

"Perfect. My teams will take over from here."

With that, the detectives assigned to the crime scene grabbed their kits and went to work, relying on their powers of observation and their skills at discerning between evidence of a crime and ordinary traces of regular activity.

"Kriven, as soon as Vidal has finished with the leg, let the dogs sniff it so they can get to work," Nico said.

Vidal and Rodon divided up the tasks, the first of which was to retrieve the limb and the second to examine the area with a fine-tooth comb.

"What about the fisherman?" Maurin asked.

"He's in a squad car on the Route de l'Asile National."

The street took its name from the Imperial Asylum of Vincennes, a charitable institution founded by Empress Eugénie for disabled workers. The park grounds had once belonged to the crown, and many kings had hunted there. The land was decreed a national treasure during the French Revolution. Later, the grounds were used for military training, and in 1900, they were the site of the summer Olympic Games. In 1945 the government returned them to recreational use.

"We'll take the fisherman," Maurin said.

Nico nodded and watched Maurin walk off with Captain Noumen. He turned to the crime scene, lifted the tape, and entered the zone, on the lookout for any evidence. Vidal had delicately removed the leg from the water and placed it on the bank and was now inspecting it closely. It was relatively intact.

"The skin is ripped, but the bone has a clean cut. I'd say a saw. In fact, I'd bet my miserable paycheck that it was a handsaw—a steel handsaw with fine triangular teeth used to cut wood. The more teeth, the smoother the cut."

A handsaw used to sever a limb. That fit seamlessly with the park's darker side. Not long ago a beautician and her partner had been accused of murdering and dismembering the parents of a baby and burying the body parts in the park. And in the nineteenth century, Louis-Auguste Papavoine was convicted of murdering two children in the Bois de Vincennes. Victor Hugo had written about him.

"How long has the leg been here?"

"The submerged part looks like it has goose bumps. The skin is wrinkled and has blisters that come off when they're touched, which means it was in the water for several hours. But it wasn't long enough for the limb to undergo substantive changes. The part that was above the water is still fresh. And look . . . here . . ."

Kriven pointed to a white mass. "Fly eggs, two to three millimeters in diameter. Just laid. So it's been here less than twenty-four hours."

"What's the angel's sex?" Nico asked.

"It's nearly impossible to tell. There's leg hair, but that doesn't prove anything. The autopsy will help us assess the victim's size, from the length of the femur, which, by the way, is not whole."

"Let's give the dogs a whiff," Nico said.

He took one last look at the leg, grateful that the local cops had had the sense to alert him. But he was getting tired of this—crazy-ass was becoming routine.

The fisherman was as pale as a ghost, and a puddle of green vomit was stinking up the space around the vehicle.

"You should walk a bit," Captain Noumen said. He helped the older man up, and they took a few unsteady steps. "What do you fish for here?"

"Carp. But I don't kill them. I throw them back after I catch them. I'm no murderer."

Noumen smiled. Now that catch would have been too easy.

"Cool," he said.

"Yes, I like just getting out and enjoying the peace and quiet."

Noumen could see that the man was finally beginning to feel better. He was no longer wobbly.

"They've ruined my spot now. I won't ever be able to go back. What if I had found a whole body? I can't even stand hurting a fish."

"Next time, you might want to take a friend."

The man nodded. "Maybe."

"So tell me, did you notice anything out of the ordinary?"

"You mean other than the leg?" The fisherman had an incredulous look on his face. "That's plenty, don't you think?"

"I'll give you that. But I was thinking about someone hanging around or anything else."

The fisherman shook his head. Suddenly he stopped in his tracks.

"I heard some barking and growling earlier. It was coming from over there," he said, looking toward the woods.

The Belgian Malinois were sniffing the leg like hungry wolves and yanking at their leashes when Nico's phone rang.

"The fisherman heard dogs fighting on the other side of the stream and some men calling them off," Maurin said.

"Ten four. We'll check it out."

Nico ended the call and passed along the message. Then he turned his attention back to the canine unit—short-haired dogs, known for their power and speed. Their ears perked, the dogs waited for the signal. Finally, Nico gave the handlers the nod, and they rushed off, following the scent of the flesh. If the rest of the body was in the woods, the dogs would find it.

15

An arm with no hand. Bite marks, probably from the dogs the fisher-man had heard.

"DNA analysis will confirm whether the arm and leg belong to the same person," Vidal told Nico.

"The two limbs seem to be similarly . . . fresh," Kriven said.

"And cut with a handsaw, it seems," Vidal added.

"Are there any distinguishing marks?" Nico asked.

"I don't see any," Kriven said.

"Over here." The voice was coming from about ten meters away.

"I'm on it," Maurin said, heading off.

Nico started in the same direction. Nobody spoke. The only sounds were the barking of the dogs and the crunching of branches and twigs underfoot.

"Chief, we've got something," Maurin called out.

Nico caught up. The canine handlers had pulled the dogs back.

"A hand."

Rodon was already getting fingerprints. He turned the palm over and manipulated the phalanges. He would rehydrate the digits in a bit of water. Then he would inject fluid into them to give them the same shape and flexibility they had when the hand was attached to a living person. He would then apply the powder and press the prints onto a white sheet of paper. He would do the same with the palm.

"I'll send Noumen over to the lab with these," Maurin said.

"Over here," came the voice of another man.

"I'll get it," Lieutenant Almeida said.

Nico turned back to the hand. The image of the autonomous hand in the *The Addams Family* popped into his head. "Same kind of cut?"

"Looks like it," Rodon said. "Clean bone cut at the wrist. Ragged skin. I'm going to see what they found over there."

"Another hand," Almeida warned.

"Rodon!" Nico yelled. "Is yours right or left?"

"Right, Chief."

"Here, too."

They could hear footsteps.

"It's a child's hand," Almeida said.

"Could it be . . ." Rodon dared to ask.

Nobody finished the sentence.

"Shit, just say it," Vidal spit out.

"Kevin Longin's right hand?" Maurin said.

A falling tree makes more noise than a growing forest, Nico thought, remembering the African proverb from somewhere. Maybe from one of Dimitri's classes.

"There's writing on the palm," Almeida said.

Vidal examined it. "It's an address. Rue de Théâtre. Not far from the Seine. Isn't there a residential hotel around there?"

"Yes," Almeida said. "A pretty big one."

"And look—there's another number: 245."

Kriven shot Captain Plassard a look. "Check it out."

Plassard grabbed his cell phone and looked up the address.

The head dog handler called out to Nico. "The dogs are running in circles. There's nothing else to find."

"Thanks. You're free to go."

Plassard looked up from the phone. "Yep, that's the hotel. Three hundred and seventy-five suites."

"Maurin, finish up here!" Nico shouted. "David, get your team. We're going to the hotel—now."

Like the dogs, he had finally gotten a good whiff.

Captain Noumen hurried into the identification lab. He spotted the police captain in charge of the eight staff members who analyzed thousands of fingerprints and palm prints every month. The job required the patience of a sphinx and excellent eyes.

"Hey, we've got a priority case here. Chief Sirsky's orders."

He handed over the sealed evidence envelope. The officer opened it and removed the fingerprints. He scanned them into his computer.

"Have a seat," he told Noumen.

Noumen did as he was told. The room was silent, except for the tapping on the keyboards. Everyone was staring at a screen.

The fingerprint examiner inspected the print's ridges and bifurcations. This was extremely precise work. Then he scanned the print into a database and launched a comparison. The French database had more than four million prints belonging to people who had committed crimes, as well as two hundred thousand unidentified prints. The machine would propose twenty-five possible matches, and the examiner would then determine if there was an actual match among them. To be valid in court, the print had to have twelve matching points and no variations.

"This will take ten to fifteen minutes."

"What's the likelihood that you'll find who they belong to?"

"We identify 30 percent of the prints we get, so roughly one in three."

If the hand belonged to a criminal, Noumen thought. Just then, the screen blinked, and twenty-five candidates popped up. With any luck, one would end the career of the handsaw killer.

Rue du Théâtre was a long one-way street that ended at a cluster of tall buildings linked by enclosed raised walkways—not the best example of modern urban architecture. The police cars braked in front of the hotel's impressive entrance. Although the building looked uninviting, it appeared to be quite popular, judging by the number of people coming and going—probably because it was a mere twenty-minute walk from the Eiffel Tower.

The sliding doors opened for Nico, and he hurried through the luxurious lobby to the ultramodern reception desk. Behind it were two women wearing navy-blue jackets and red scarves. One looked up and smiled. Nico pulled out his badge.

"I'd like to know if room 245 is occupied."

The woman typed into the computer, her fingers trembling. Seeing her anxiety, the other woman answered for her.

"Yes, it was booked for a week."

"Since when?"

"Saturday."

"And by whom?"

"Someone named Fritz Haarmann."

"Can you spell that, please?"

She spelled the name.

"What type of room is it?"

"It's a two-room, fifty-five-square-meter suite," the first reception-ist said. "There's a bedroom with a king-size bed, a living room with a large-screen television, a fully equipped kitchen area, and a bathroom with a bathtub and separate WC."

She knew her rooms by heart.

"How did Mr. Haarmann pay?"

"In cash."

"How much?"

"The apartment goes for 240 euros a night. Times seven nights, that comes to 1,680 euros."

"Has anyone from your staff gone into the apartment since Saturday?"

"Mr. Haarmann said he didn't want the apartment cleaned. Housecleaning was scheduled for the end of his stay."

"Thank you."

They both smiled.

"It was a pleasure, sir," the first one said. "Have a good day."

The two women turned back to their computers.

Nico leaned over the counter. "Sorry, I'm not done yet. I need to get into that suite. And to do that, I need a key card."

"Sir, that suite is still occupied," the second receptionist said. "We can't let you in."

Nico flashed them a reassuring smile and then said firmly, "This is a police investigation."

As he said this, the women looked to their right. He followed their gaze and spotted a man in a suit heading their way. Most likely, he was the manager.

"Can I help you?" he asked as soon as he reached the desk.

"Chief Nico Sirsky. We need to get into room 245."

"Of course." The man turned around and fetched a key card. He frowned at the receptionists and smiled at Nico. "We're at your service, Inspector."

"Thank you. Please don't inform any of your guests of our presence or do anything that could interfere with the investigation." He looked at the two receptionists, whose expressions made them look like scolded children.

"Which elevator?" he asked.

"Over there," the women blurted in unison, pointing in the same direction.

"What floor?"

"Twenty-second."

Nico turned around. "Two men on the stairs, the others with me."

Captain Plassard headed toward the stairs, taking another team member with him. Kriven hit the button for the elevator, while Nico called Maurin.

"The suite was reserved in the name of a Fritz Haarmann—that's two *a*'s and two *n*'s. He paid cash. See what you can find out."

The elevator doors opened like the jaws of a shark.

"We're heading up to the suite now."

"Be careful."

They filed into the elevator.

"What did she say?" Kriven asked.

"'Be careful.'"

"Be careful?" Vidal said. "When was the last time we took that advice seriously?"

"At lunch the day before yesterday, when you wanted to order oysters with mignonette sauce at that hole in the wall," Almeida said. "Aren't you glad you exercised proper caution?"

"Yeah, you got a point," Vidal said. "The way those oysters looked, I could have wound up sick as a dog."

Nico didn't say anything and just stared at the elevator doors. He had a bad feeling that they'd all be feeling sicker than a dog in the next couple of minutes.

He had done it perfectly. It was a masterpiece. In the end, killing wasn't so difficult. It was an exercise in style. He had to admit that he liked it. No, *like* wasn't a strong enough word. He had felt an extraordinary shiver, an adrenaline surge. Fritz Haarmann, Hanover, 1923. A thrilling trip back in time. A little history lesson. He'd done his part.

But had he fulfilled his own fantasies or just copied those of another? Did his pleasure come from the perfect execution of his mission or from the depths of his soul? How could he know?

"Hi," he said, arriving at his destination.

He sat down at their table. Some were focused on their screens. Others glanced at him discreetly. What did they see? Could they tell how different he was now?

Number 245. Nico knocked. Nothing. He waved to Kriven, who held out the key card. Nico and the other team members pulled out their semiautomatic 9mm SIG Sauers and prepared to breach the door. After a glance around and a nod, he kicked it open, and they swept into the suite like shadows.

When the odor hit him, Nico's knees buckled. He stopped breathing just long enough to collect himself. Then, arms straight and gun in front of him, he entered the bedroom.

The sopping sheets gleamed in the sunshine streaming through the picture window. The scarlet fluid was pooled on the floor.

Nico heard raspy breathing to his right.

"Almeida, if you're going to lose your breakfast, please do it outside," he said.

His own heart was racing.

"I'll be okay, Chief."

"You know nobody will hold it against you."

"Apartment clear!" Kriven yelled. "You need to see the living room. It's a real slaughterhouse."

From the hallway, they heard Plassard. "Is it over? Did we miss it?" He hadn't seen anything yet. A few seconds later they heard him again. "Shit."

"Is that the best you can do?" Vidal asked. "How about, 'Holy mother of all shit!'?"

Nico knew exactly what Vidal was trying to do. But in this carnage, nothing could lighten the mood. He couldn't stop staring at the bloody bed. Almeida's gaze, however, was fixed elsewhere.

"Chief, there's something on the wall."

"'All for three round . . . coins,'" Nico read out loud.

It was the same red ink and spidery handwriting. What had Małgorzata Włodarczyk, the Polish professor, said? "Down the chimney comes Santa Claus. But where, oh where, are all the toys? In his big bag, at the bottom . . . One by one here they come: one piglet fair, two teddy bears, three round balloons in tow, four planes a pretty lemon yellow, five yummy candies—oh!"

It should have been "three round balloons," but the bastard had changed it up. A small dish holding three euro coins was on the bed. Three round coins. But that wasn't all.

"Chief!" It was Kriven, who had come up behind Nico and, in turn, discovered the decapitated head. It had been carefully placed on the sheet with its eyes wide open.

"What kind of lunatic would do this?" Kriven asked.

Once again, Nico had no answer. He turned to Almeida.

"That looks like a bite on the neck, doesn't it?"

Almeida holstered his gun and inspected the wound. "Let me get my kit."

"There are body parts in the living room," Kriven said. "And . . . You've got to come see it for yourself."

Nico followed Kriven into the living room and kitchen area. His eyes were immediately drawn to the panoramic view of the capital. The room was ultramodern: flat-screen television, fake wood flooring, a sofa upholstered in a geometric pattern, chrome finishes. He spotted an open bottle of Moët & Chandon, but just one glass. The killer probably took his so he wouldn't leave any evidence. But why had he bothered, if he had bitten the victim?

"The table is set for two," Plassard said.

"And the main course is ready to be served." Kriven pointed to a piece of nauseating offal.

"Brain," Vidal said. "Some old-timers still eat it, and you can get it at most butcher shops."

"Almeida?" Nico called out. "Can you tell me if the skull is intact?"

With that, they heard Almeida running down the hall to throw up in a trash can.

"Well, clearly, this dude is out of his mind," Vidal said.

And the victim was a dude, too. His penis lay on the coffee table.

"Plassard, go take care of the hotel," Nico said. "The rest of you, get to work. Get everything you can here, and then we'll have the morgue pick up what remains of the body. I want you questioning people on this floor. The message is obvious: this is our copycat. I want your undivided attention on this. Remember, we've got the second right hand found in the Bois de Vincennes—a child's hand, and I'm betting it belongs to Kevin Longin. The killer is leaving bread crumbs. He wants us to know it's him. He's playing a game, and right now, he's the one marking the trail. Let's get a move on."

The fingerprint examiner scrolled through the possible matches. Each had a score based on the convergence between the recorded fingerprint and the adult hand found in the Bois de Vincennes, but the software didn't have the final say. Now it was up to the examiner, who was comparing the results.

"It looks like we've found him," he said, printing up an identification report.

Noumen was pacing. They weren't done yet. The two men moved into the next room, where the paper fingerprint cards were stored. It felt like Ali Baba's cave. The examiner found the card in question and returned to the first room, where he placed it in a projector. The two fingerprint samples were enlarged on the screen, and the examiner began a manual comparison of the whorls and lines. It was important to be absolutely sure, as any error could bring an entire criminal investigation into question.

Noumen got lost for a while in the twists and turns on the screen, unable to make out the similarities and differences. He felt nauseated. How did this man do it all day long?

"It's him, without a doubt," the examiner said, with the first indication of any emotion in his voice.

Commander Maurin swallowed hard in the silence of the office. She grabbed her phone and called her immediate superior, Deputy Chief Rost.

"What did you find?" he asked without preamble.

"Fritz Haarmann is the Butcher of Hanover. Our copycat is having the time of his life, I'd say."

16

Tanya emerged from the Faidherbe-Chaligny metro station. Directly across the street was Saint Antoine Hospital, flanked by a bar and a café. The hospital was a registered historical landmark, and Tanya, an architect, had long admired the building's design, with its arched entrance and courtyard.

She passed under the French flag and the inscription *"Liberté, égalité, fraternité,"* and headed toward the Jacques Caroli Building. She hurried past the gift shop and cafeteria, glancing at the tired and anxious faces of visitors grabbing coffee and a bite to eat before returning to their loved ones' rooms.

Not long ago, Tanya had been just as tired and anxious as the people she observed now. A heart condition had almost killed Anya, and she had spent a great deal of time in the hospital. Nico and Tanya had already lost their father. She would always remember the sadness in their father's eyes—a deep sorrow, because he knew he was leaving them, and the sorrow was greater than his physical pain.

Tanya felt lucky to have a brother like Nico. They had been close since childhood. When they were kids, he was her champion, but then, when he began having troubles with Sylvie, she became his protector. She had watched over him during Sylvie's crazy ups and downs, the separation, the divorce, and his transition to single parenthood. Nico didn't deserve what had happened to him. He was a good man. And she was ecstatic when Nico and Caroline clicked.

Caroline and Tanya's husband, Alexis, had gone to medical school together. He'd sent Nico to her for an ulcer that had reappeared. Caroline was why she was here today. Nico was literally scared sick that he had done something to alienate her, and Tanya was hoping that a lunch date would enable her to allay her brother's fears.

She climbed the stairs to the gastroenterology department that Caroline headed up. Right away, she spotted Caroline in her white lab coat, talking with a nurse at the end of the hallway. Nico had chosen a woman who looked very different from the Sirskys. Tanya's hair was long and blond; Caroline's was brown and she wore it in a stylish short cut. Tanya and Nico had clear blue eyes; Caroline's were dark and deep.

Caroline waved to Tanya and gave the nurse a nod, indicating they were done. As she started down the hallway, Tanya once again admired Caroline's bearing, which was as straight as a ballerina's.

"Let me get rid of this lab coat, and I'll be right with you. I reserved a table at L'Abribus."

The quiet bistro with Mediterranean décor was a short walk from the hospital and a popular lunch spot for hospital staff. Their table was on the veranda, with a view of the busy street. Once they were seated, and Tanya could get a better look at Caroline, she couldn't help but pick up the change in her face. Caroline was paler than usual, and her features were tense.

"You seem fatigued," Tanya said. "Are you getting enough sleep?"

"Yes, I'm fine . . . There's just a lot going on at the hospital. Potential doctors to interview, tough cases. You know."

This wasn't going to be easy. Caroline was too smart to be tricked into revealing something she wasn't ready to divulge.

"Nico told me you were looking tired."

Caroline gave Tanya a weak smile. The waiter arrived with their *bruschettas au saumon fumé.*

Tanya would have to try a new tactic.

"Has Dimitri started getting ready for his finals? It won't be long before school's out."

"A bit. He started studying last weekend."

"He's really come to rely on you."

"It's not a problem. And Nico is always there for him."

"He's found a mother in you who's much more involved in his life than his own mother. But it couldn't have been easy—becoming an instant parent to a teenage boy."

"Dimitri isn't the problem!"

Caroline's tone startled Tanya. Her friend had never been sharp like that with her before.

"That's good to hear," Tanya said, smiling to ease the tension. "I'm glad to hear that. You know he loves you."

"How are Lana and Bogdan?"

Caroline was trying to shift the attention off her. She saw Tanya's children often enough to know how they were doing.

"They're fine. Keeping their grades up."

"Dimitri said Bogdan got Anya's computer set up in no time. He knew exactly what he was doing. They would have been lost without him."

Tanya's heart warmed, and she nodded. She was proud of her son. Tanya was sure that Caroline watched over Dimitri, too. Did she feel the same kind of maternal pride, though? Tanya couldn't say.

"They would have gotten it set up eventually," Tanya said. "Bogdan is just a natural-born geek. He wants to be a pilot, but I'm wondering if he would make a better software architect or security engineer. Who knows?"

"He certainly is smart enough. And Lana—there's another bright one. She wants to be a doctor."

"Like her father and you. Now that she knows you, she wants it even more. You're her role model." That was another way of telling Caroline how important she was to their family. "And of course, Dimitri is aiming to join the police, much to Nico's dismay."

Caroline's face softened, and Tanya caught a look in her eyes. Yes, she did love the boy like a mother.

"Nico vacillates between being afraid something will happen to him and being proud," Caroline said. "But nothing is set in stone, and Dimitri has plenty of time to change his mind."

"Like my two kids."

As Tanya finished her salmon, she noticed that Caroline had barely touched hers. She had just fiddled with it, pushing the fish from one side of her plate to the other. The waiter cleared the dishes.

"Aren't you hungry?"

"No . . . not really . . . It's hot."

The waiter brought over two servings of the famous house tiramisu.

"You don't seem to be feeling well, Caroline. I understand why Nico's worried."

"Is that why we're having lunch?"

Now it was Tanya's tone that was sharp. "Nico's never arranged our lunches."

"Sure, but he did ask you to get together with me and find out what you could." It wasn't a question.

"It wasn't like that," Tanya said, ignoring Caroline's not-so-subtle rebuke. "I want to tell you a little story. Has Nico ever told you what he said to Alexis the day we got married?"

"No."

"Nico pulled Alexis aside and told him that he expected him to be 100 percent committed. If Alexis didn't pour everything he had into our marriage, he'd be dealing with a very angry brother-in-law—one with a gun."

Tanya shook her head and wiped her lips. Caroline said nothing.

"That's my Nico," Tanya continued. "Loyal to the bone. He wasn't joking."

She paused, noting the surprise on Caroline's face. Just what she wanted. She swooped in for the kill.

"Thing is, Caroline, I'm just as loyal to my brother. He's a good man who happens to be crazy about you. I'd do anything to protect him. I may not have a weapon, but in the end, that's just a detail."

17

Deputy Commissioner Cohen nodded, and Nico called everyone into his office.

Judge Becker was the first to arrive, followed by Dominique Kreiss, Deputy Chief Rost, and his three squad leaders: Kriven, Maurin, and Théron. They all took seats at Nico's table, where there were enough bottles of water and plastic glasses for the eight of them. It was unusually hot for May, and they would have gladly exchanged their professional attire for shorts, if the dress policy had permitted it.

Cohen looked at Becker. "Judge, why don't you start."

"We have four victims now, and a killer somewhere out there," Becker said. "Let's not forget that the nursery rhyme in the anonymous letter suggests that other victims will follow."

"We don't have anything more on the letter sent to the commissioner, other than the fact that the burner used by the writer pinged off a cell tower near Square de Montholon in the eleventh arrondissement," Commander Théron said. "None of the neighbors saw anything."

"We know who the two teddy bears and the little piglet are," Nico said. "Our copycat's fourth victim, whose leg was found at the

Bois de Vincennes, was a homeless young man known to the police. Commander Maurin?"

"Noë Valles, age twenty, picked up several times for public solicitation. He was dismembered with a handsaw, and his body parts were left in the Bois de Vincennes and the suite at the hotel. The reservation was made over the phone, and the person who took the suite paid in cash."

Nico stood up and walked over to the wall maps. He added pins for the two new crime scenes.

"The autopsy is underway," Kriven said. "They've already run DNA tests to make sure all the body parts, except the second right hand, belonged to Noë Valles. The DNA tests also concluded that that hand belonged to Kevin Longin. The killer left a message in red ink: 'All for three round coins,' along with a small dish containing three euro coins."

"I'm meeting with the prefect this afternoon," Cohen said. "What am I supposed to tell him? That this killer is taking us for a ride?"

"We're looking for witnesses around Montparnasse who may have seen Valles with the killer," Nico said.

"So you think the copycat could have approached him there?" Becker asked.

"Why not? It seems his objective is to stick as close as possible to his famous role models."

"Yes, I want to talk about the killers he's imitating," Cohen said.

"Clearly, he wants to copy the best," Nico said. "First, the Ukrainian, Andrei Chikatilo, the Butcher of Rostov, with fifty-two victims including fourteen girls around Juliette Bisot's age. His specialties—knifing, mutilation, and cannibalism. *Segundo*: the Swede Thomas Quick, who claimed to dismember his victims' bodies and keep their body parts as trophies. Third, Lucian Staniak, the Red Spider, who wrote letters to the cops. He targeted young women, had sadosexual relations with them, and eviscerated them. He also committed some of his crimes on a holiday, and Eva Keller was killed on Ascension Day. What can you add, Maurin?"

"Noë Valles's murder was patterned after those of Fritz Haarmann, the Butcher of Hanover. Haarmann murdered twenty-four young men between 1918 and 1924. He was a cannibal and a vampire—he liked to bite his victims on the neck. He cut up the bodies and threw some of the parts into the Leine River. The rest he cooked up and ate. Haarmann was executed—beheaded on a guillotine—in 1925."

"Russia, Sweden, Poland, and Germany," Nico said. "He's mapped it all out."

"He must have made some small mistake!" Cohen said, his face turning red.

"I think we should be looking at how he met his victims," Nico said. "And we should go in order. Who got close to the Bisot family before their daughter was kidnapped? We need to find Kevin Longin's mysterious friend, along with Eva Keller's Wilde. And we should investigate Montparnasse, where Noë Valles hung out."

"Fine," Cohen said, turning to Dominique Kreiss. "Can you give us a profile?"

"Our killer is, indeed, fascinated with his idols, but not everyone who's fascinated with serial killers becomes a murderer. If that were the case, we'd be in real trouble. A person who'd do this sort of thing has irrepressible drives and fantasies. Our man is a psychopath who looks stable and healthy. He's especially intelligent, and he inspires trust. Of course, he's a sadist, and his sadism goes hand in hand with highly ritualized behavior. Eviscerating and dismembering his victims reinforces his supremacy. He needs more than the kill to heal his lack of recognition, his narcissistic wound."

"Why the imitation?" Maurin asked.

"He wants to prove he's equal to the masters. His attitude demonstrates pathological narcissism, a feeling of omnipotence. Malignant narcissists have an exaggerated sense of their own importance. He is arrogant, has a thirst for power, and feels an excessive need to be admired, most notably by people with status. He has no empathy."

"Thus Oscar Wilde," Théron said.

"Certainly. Oscar Wilde symbolizes a cynical and elegant dandy. He developed the theme of duplicity in his only novel, *The Picture of Dorian Gray*. In it, Wilde describes the moral decline of a young man who's pursuing a life of self-indulgent sensuality, and he winds up murdering a friend who has learned just how corrupt he is. Here's a quote: 'To love oneself is the beginning of a lifelong romance.' That's pure narcissism."

"So, our man is a narcissist who looks perfectly rational, but underneath it all has a pathological need to kill in a way that proves his intelligence and superiority," Cohen said. "What else do we know about him?"

"Like most sadistic killers, he knows how to recruit and charm his victims and how to remove the evidence once he's killed them. He's methodical and calculating. But that won't keep him from making a mistake."

"He's narcissistic, sadistic, and methodical," Becker said. "He's also right-handed and wears a size 44 shoe. Now all we need is his address."

Kreiss ignored the crack. Becker was as frustrated as the rest of them. "Serial killers usually live near their first crime scene."

"Louviers, in Normandy," Nico said. "But Paris is the theater for his crimes, so he has some connection to this city."

"There's the theory of the flight of the bumblebee," Kreiss said.

Nico raised an eyebrow. "You can't possibly mean Rimsky-Korsakov's *The Flight of the Bumblebee*."

Nico was intimately familiar with the orchestral interlude written for the opera *The Tale of Tsar Saltan*, which was based on Alexander Pushkin's poem of adventure and love. Anya had often recited the poem to him when he was a child. He would always snuggle closer to her when the kite circled over the swan: "Talons spread, and bloodstained beak." Then he would cheer when the tsar's arrow struck it down.

"No, I'm referring to a study at Queen Mary University of London on bumblebee behavior. The researchers found that bees don't forage close to their hives, because they want to keep predators and parasites away from their nest. The rational-choice theory of geographic profiling integrates this idea of a buffer zone. It serves to protect the killer's home or place of work."

Nico turned his attention to the map of Paris. "If we connect the crime scenes—Montmartre in the north, Square de Montholon and the La Grange aux Belles Middle School to the east, the Bois de Vincennes to the southeast, and the Montparnasse station and the hotel to the south and southwest—then we can deduce that the copycat spends the better part of his time in this sector." Nico pointed to the central zone. "It's not much to go on, but let's keep that in mind."

"Anything else?" Cohen asked, looking around the table before turning to Nico. "You've got that look, Nico."

"I'm just wondering if the room number at the hotel means anything."

Dominique Kreiss gasped. "Room 245—four for the fourth crime, Noë Valles."

"Two for Kevin Longin," Nico said. "The second murder."

"And five to announce another one," Kreiss said.

"Do you think he left a clue?" Cohen asked.

"A clue that we missed," Nico murmured.

18

One piglet fair, two teddy bears, three round balloons in tow, four planes a pretty lemon yellow, and five yummy candies—oh!

Nico was worried about a fifth and then a sixth murder. And then what? Could they stop the killer in time? Or would he just disappear as suddenly as he had appeared? He was the gamemaster. But as smart and passionate as their man was, as much as he wanted to emulate his idols down to their exact choice of prey, Nico sensed that his need to kill was becoming frenetic. Were the copycat's own demons beginning to govern him?

His phone buzzed. It was Tanya. He didn't bother with any pleasantries.

"Did you talk to Caroline?"

"Well, you're on edge, aren't you. To answer your question, yes, we talked."

"So?"

"Listen, she didn't tell me anything, but I got the feeling that something has happened. She seems vulnerable and scared."

"Scared? Of what?"

"I don't know what it is, Nico. But I wouldn't be worried about her feelings for you. She's obviously still in love with you."

"But she's been pushing me away. What if there's someone else? I'm losing it, Tanya. What would I do without her?"

"Quit worrying about that. She adores you and Dimitri and wants to be with you two."

"I just can't be sure, Tanya. The other day she told me she wasn't Dimitri's mother. What was that about?"

"I don't know, Nico. You've just got to talk to her. I can't believe you haven't already. You face every other issue in your life head-on. So sit down with her. That's the only way you'll find out what's going on. She's too loyal to you to tell anyone else what she's feeling."

Nico sighed. She was right.

"A little more sisterly advice: don't put it off. Caroline's not in great shape. She's lost all her color, and she didn't eat a bite of her food."

What was she hiding? Nico's hand trembled as he opened a desk drawer and pulled out his ulcer medication. Just as Caroline hadn't told him what was eating at her, he hadn't said anything about the gnawing in his gut.

"Keep me posted, Nico. Promise?"

"Yes, Tanya. Thanks."

Nico heard her blow him a kiss, a good-bye ritual they had followed since childhood. He swallowed a pill and looked at his watch. Maurin and Noumen were on their way to Normandy to check into the Bisot family connection. He called Kriven into his office.

"Chief, Captain Plassard's hitting the restrooms at the Montparnasse train station to see if he can turn up anything on Valles." The restrooms were a hot spot for exhibitionists and general riffraff.

"Good. You're going back to the hotel?"

"That's right . . . Um, I was thinking of taking Ms. Kreiss along."

Nico sized up his commander and didn't say anything. He'd seen that Kriven and Kreiss were attracted to each other. So now that Kriven was divorcing Clara, would he be getting it on with Kreiss?

"I believe she's busy elsewhere," Nico finally said. "Sorry about that."

The body parts in room 245 had been removed and sent to the morgue, but otherwise, everything remained untouched. The room had been sealed off, and an officer was guarding the door. Kriven, Vidal, and Almeida snapped on their gloves and began searching the room, carefully avoiding the puddles of blood. They hadn't found anything before, but they had to try again.

After several minutes, Vidal spoke. "Kriven, come over here."

"Got something?"

"An invitation to go dancing." With that, he jiggled his hips.

Captain Plassard took in the Montparnasse train station, which opened in 1840 and was renovated in 1852, then rebuilt from scratch in 1969. General Dietrich von Choltitz, the Nazi military governor of Paris, surrendered to General Philippe Leclerc there on August 25, 1944. The newest incarnation was a bustling hub lined with offices and shops and boasted a skyscraper, the Tour Montparnasse. On clear days, the view from the fifty-ninth floor extended forty kilometers in every direction. But Plassard wasn't there as a tourist.

He and two other detectives from his squad weaved their way through the crowded main hall, which reeked of fast food, sweat, and dust. It reminded Plassard of something Commissaire San-Antonio—the main character in a crime series by French author Frédéric Dard—had once said: "Life is gray, with all these grimy people who look like dripping umbrellas." Dard, one of France's best-selling postwar writers, was a favorite of Plassard's. San-Antonio was also the author's pseudonym, which he had chosen by closing his eyes and pointing at a map of the world. His finger landed on the city of San Antonio, Texas—which was very far from where they were now.

"You take the gardens," Plassard said, pointing to one of the detectives. He turned to the other one. "And you scope out the waiting rooms, while I'll check out the upstairs bathrooms. You both have pictures of Noë Valles. Show them around, and ask questions. Dig up something we can run with."

Plassard took the escalator, scanning the hall as he ascended. He entered the men's room. He knew from his time on the vice squad that it was a heavily frequented pickup spot. He stepped into a stall and aimed for the toilet. Good thing Kriven wasn't around. He'd never hear the end of it. He took his time, studying the wall separating his stall from the next one over until he found the glory hole, an opening used for spying and anonymous blow jobs. He spotted a shadow through it and then a dilated pupil, followed by a finger inviting him closer. As he moved closer, he heard a moan of satisfaction from the other side. He pulled back and held his badge up to the hole. That was a lot less enticing.

"Police. Come on out."

"Please, I didn't mean any harm. I'm married. I've got kids."

"Listen, I'm not from vice. I just want to show you a picture of a prostitute who works around here. We need some information. That's all."

Plassard and the man stepped out of their respective stalls. The man was wearing a suit and tie and was carrying a briefcase.

"I'll try to help," he said, looking sheepish.

"His name is Noë Valles," Plassard said, holding up the photo. "Does he look familiar?"

"I don't come here often, you know . . ."

If the man kept treating him like an idiot, he'd have to scare him.

"Maybe you forget faces, but surely you remember cocks. Is that it?"
The man's face went white. He was ready to talk.

Olivier Pons and Marc Drillan, friends of Eva Keller, were twenty-three and twenty-four, respectively. To impress them, Commander Théron had the gates opened for him, and he parked his vehicle inside the courtyard. It worked. The kids' legs were shaking as they made their way into police headquarters.

Théron and two other detectives led them to the top floor. He let the chief's secretary know they had arrived before settling them in the interrogation rooms at the end of the hall. Nico would be there soon. He wanted in on the action. Théron appreciated having a boss who fought alongside his foot soldiers.

It was easy to feel claustrophobic in these tiny and cramped rooms, each of which had only a table, some chairs, a computer, and a camera. Every interrogation was recorded and filmed. It was also transcribed and written up as a report—which was an incredible waste of time. A uniformed officer, called a ghost, was always stationed in a corner during an interrogation. The ghost's role was to watch and intervene in case the questioning got out of hand.

Vidal held out the invitation. The Palace Jazz Band would be playing at the Paris Bar Association, located in a magnificent building next to police headquarters. Was the invitation meant for them? Was the killer provoking them? Kriven felt his blood start to boil.

"It says June 21. That's ages away," Vidal said, reading his thoughts.

"What does he think we're going to do till then?" Kriven growled. "Twiddle our thumbs?"

"Damn it. It's the bar association! That's like setting an appointment in the middle of a wasp's nest."

They were sure it was a clue they had missed earlier. They had found the invitation stuck under some plates in the kitchen cupboard. That it was in the kitchen was enough to confirm their suspicions.

"What if our copycat is one of the wasps?" Almeida asked.

Vidal closed the cupboard door. "That would make the world an even crappier place than it already is."

Nico sat down across from Marc Drillan, the older of Eva's friends.

"I'm Chief Sirsky, head of the Paris Criminal Investigation Division. I asked my commander to bring you here because I wanted to meet you in person."

Drillan nodded.

"How long had you known Eva?"

"Since we started at La Fémis two years ago."

"Did you get together when you weren't in class?"

"Sometimes we had lunch between classes or went to student events, but nothing more than that."

"Did you ever go to her place?"

"Yes, to study."

"And Olivier Pons?"

"The same."

"Did either of you ever date her?"

"Olivier is living with his girlfriend. He wasn't interested in Eva."

"What about you?"

Drillan's jaw tightened, and he curled his hands into fists—a classic angry reaction, usually accompanied by a faster heartbeat and a rise in temperature. Nico saw his opening.

"You liked Eva, didn't you? But she didn't have the same feelings for you, is that it?"

"She had her opportunity, but let's just say she passed it up."

"Why?"

He shrugged. He was as taut as a bow.

"Did she meet someone else?"

"I don't know. She didn't share that kind of thing with me."

"What about the documentary?"

Drillan slouched in his chair and crossed his arms in a defensive pose.

"Why did you choose that subject matter? Why serial killers?"

"Why not?"

"Surely there were more pleasant topics to focus on."

"It was a documentary."

"Of course. But a rather morbid one, don't you think?"

"Maybe so. But everyone loves watching serial killers on TV and in the movies. Everybody's fascinated with psycho killers. People invent bogeymen to scare the hell out of themselves and religion to make them feel safe."

He spit out his tirade like a half-chewed mouthful. Who did he want to impress? Nico or himself?

"So was it your idea? Remember, we have Olivier right here to confirm what you say."

The boy was as white as a sheet. He licked his lips.

"That's not what I said."

Nico stared at him.

"It was Eva's idea."

"And did you think it was a good one?"

"At first we wanted to do something else—*The Digital Revolution: What if Cinema's Losing Its Memory?* What does the replacement of film stock with digital technology mean for the art as a whole? It's a hot topic these days."

"And a very different one from serial killers. What made you change your mind?"

"We weren't all that keen on it at first, but Eva was convinced that this was what we should be doing and she talked us into going along with her plan."

"How?"

Drillan squirmed in his chair.

"She was way more talented than us. Brilliant, in fact. She was raised with cameras all around her."

"In other words, she would guarantee your success."

"Working with someone like her can open doors."

"So where were you in your project?"

Drillan blushed. "It was coming along . . ."

"I imagine the deadline isn't that far off."

"In three weeks."

"I'd like to see it."

"Eva was the one who had it," he said, shifting in his chair.

"Don't you have a copy?"

"Eva didn't want anyone else to see it."

Nico was sure they had let her do all the work. "And you haven't worked on it since her death?"

"It's been hard. We've all been in shock over what happened to her."

"I understand. Did you hope to get your deadline extended?"

Drillan lowered his gaze. "Well, the situation would justify it, don't you think?"

"But the dean of the school has rejected your request. Isn't that right?"

"That's right."

"Are you going to continue working on the same topic?"

"We haven't decided yet. Frankly, we're a little . . . lost."

"Is it you or the video recording that's lost?"

Drillan chewed the inside of his cheek.

"The memory card," he finally said.

"And you have no idea where it is?"

"I guess at Eva's."

"What exactly is on it?"

"Well, our interviews, for one thing. We discussed how serial killers like Hannibal Lecter are depicted as extremely intelligent and manipulative, when, in reality, they're more ordinary. And in the movies and on television, the police always catch the bad guys, which isn't actually the case."

"Don't you have anything better to show for all the time you spent on this project?" Nico asked.

Drillan swallowed. "Serial killers represent only one percent of the prison population, but with all the media attention they get, you'd think they were everywhere. We were planning to look at the mediatization of the phenomenon. You know—crime sells."

"Nothing new there. I would have thought that Eva Keller was capable of doing better than that. But perhaps you weren't?"

"I . . . How can you . . ."

"I can tell a slacker when I see one, young man. Who do you think you're talking to? Stop playing games right now!"

"Wait a sec! I don't understand! Just because I don't know what Eva did with the video—"

"Have you even seen what she did? This is what I think: you're a first-rate phony, and you're going to fail because you don't have anything to turn in."

"It's her fault! Eva wanted to control everything."

"That was convenient, wasn't it? She did the work, and you were going to share the credit."

"She wanted to get started on her own, to develop the idea. She said she'd show us soon, once she'd worked out some of the details."

"A turnkey project produced by William Keller's daughter. How were you going to explain that to your professors once they found out?"

"Shit! We had a good topic. Then she went and changed it and wanted to do it all herself. She told us she had some juicy information from a first-rate source."

"Who was that?"

"Some guy she met."

"What's his name?"

"I don't know! She said she needed to protect him."

"Wilde? Does that sound familiar at all?"

"Other than Oscar, no."

There he was again. What if her friend's first name was Oscar, and she'd called him Wilde to keep his name a secret?

"Her informant clearly knew a great deal about criminals. Do you have any idea who it could be?"

"We attended a conference at the university just before Christmas."

"What kind of conference?"

"'The Abuse of Truth'—it covered a lot. It explored the interplay of truth and deception in the world of psychology and law."

"Did they talk about serial killers?"

"Yes."

"Did Eva participate?"

"She mostly listened, like we all did."

"Did anyone in particular attract her attention?"

"There was a guy . . ."

"One of the speakers?"

"No, a student from the law school. He kept asking questions."

"Can you describe him?"

"Not really. Brown hair, brown eyes. Ordinary looking. Oh—he was wearing cologne. It smelled fancy. I can't tell you anything else."

"Did Eva talk to him?"

"Yeah, for a while when the conference was over. I asked if she wanted me to wait for her, and she said no."

"Did you hear anything about him afterward? Or about an Oscar or a Wilde?"

"No, nothing. But Eva was always secretive. When she needed to be, she was as quiet as a tomb."

That was a bad choice of words.

Louviers was a pretty Normandy port town with a population of eighteen thousand people. Commander Charlotte Maurin and Captain Ayoub Noumen were there to meet with Juliette Bisot's parents at the mother's office. They walked there from the train station.

"If we ask the right questions, we may be lucky enough to get a lead," Maurin said as Noumen opened the door to the building.

"I hope so, Commander."

Dr. Bisot offered the two detectives some tea, and when they declined, she indicated two chairs where they could sit. Noumen noted that the father seemed to be no more than a shadow.

"Did you meet anyone new in the period leading up to your daughter's disappearance?" Maurin asked once they were settled in.

"Not really," the mother said, holding her head high.

"Did any of your patients show unwarranted interest in your private life?"

"I don't mix business with pleasure."

"And you, Mr. Bisot? Did you have any new customers?" Noumen asked.

"Of course. I run a business, so I meet people every day."

"You didn't notice anything suspicious?"

"Nothing. Believe me. I've thought about it every day for the last four months . . . until they found Juliette."

"Did anybody you know take a sudden interest in your daughter?" Maurin asked.

Dr. Bisot let out a weary sigh. "We've been asked these questions a thousand times."

"Do you know anyone who splits his time between Louviers and Paris? Or someone who goes to the capital often?"

"Louviers is only a hundred kilometers from Paris," Mr. Bisot said, his tone sharp. "We've got friends who go back and forth all the time."

"You also have a nephew at school in Paris, is that right?"

"He's studying law there," Dr. Bisot said. "He was planning to specialize in trade law, but now, with what's happened to Juliette, he's talking about criminal law."

"What year is he in?"

"He's finishing his undergraduate studies and has applied for a master's degree in law and forensic science. But why all these questions about Etienne?"

"No reason," Noumen said. "We're just trying to get the full picture, ma'am."

"Don't tell me you came all this way for no reason! I have a hard time believing that."

"We think that the person who kidnapped Juliette—"

"And murdered her," Mr. Bisot broke in.

"And murdered her, yes . . . We think that person knows you and had a reason for choosing Juliette. Chief Sirsky already told you that the killer was looking for a very specific kind of victim. We also think that he may split his time between Louviers and Paris."

"Which would explain why he committed other crimes in the capital," Dr. Bisot said.

"Exactly."

"Even if you're right, I don't see what that has to do with Etienne."

"Perhaps nothing directly, but we have to explore all possible avenues," Noumen said. "What else can you tell us about the boy?"

"Etienne Delamare is my sister's son—her only child. He's twenty, and he's both brilliant and charming," Mr. Bisot said. "Juliette's death has been even harder on him than it's been on our own son."

"That's because your son's just three years old, right?" Noumen said. "Not old enough yet to really understand. Do your sister and brother-in-law still live in Louviers?"

"Yes, my sister teaches history at the high school, and my brother-in-law is in local politics."

"And where is Etienne right now?"

"He's in Paris. His exams are coming up."

"Do you know anyone named Wilde? Or perhaps an Oscar?"

The Bisots shook their heads.

"A friend of Etienne's, perhaps?" Noumen pressed.

"Leave Etienne out of this, please." Mr. Bisot was angry now. "Our family has suffered enough."

Maurin persisted. "Did he ever mention the name Eva Keller?"

"Good God! How dare you? I myself go to Paris regularly for business! You might as well accuse me while you're at it!"

"Dear . . ."

"No! I want these people out of here right now! Get them out of my sight, or else—"

"Or else what?" asked Captain Noumen.

"Or else I'll take care of you myself! I've got nothing to lose now."

Noumen looked over at Dr. Bisot. Tears were flowing down her cheeks.

19

Andrei, Thomas, Lucian, Fritz . . . Each one an inspiration. He had studied their crimes down to the smallest detail. He had copied them perfectly, determined for his murders to be exactly like the original works of art. He would be remembered as a forger who excelled in reproducing crimes. Because he was Louis, the gamemaster—a monster with several heads. He was Cerberus, the monstrous multiheaded dog that guarded the underworld, keeping anyone from leaving. Cerberus was usually described as having three heads—the past, the present, and the future— but the Greek poet Hesiod had given him fifty, while the poet Pindar had endowed him with a hundred. It didn't matter. He was Andrei, Thomas, Lucian, and Fritz—and so many others—all in one. He was Louis, the gamemaster. Someday he would have many fanatical admirers.

"He's got nerve, leaving an invitation for an event at the Paris Bar Association," Judge Becker said. His features were drawn, and his eyes were heavy with fatigue. "Are you absolutely sure it's a message from the killer?"

"The invitation was hidden in a cupboard in his hotel suite," Nico said.

"And you're telling me that Eva Keller was working on a documentary with a law student she met at a conference, and Juliette Bisot had a cousin studying law in Paris."

"We showed Etienne Delamare's photo to the two students at her school, but they didn't recognize him."

"That would have made it too easy, I suppose."

"He's got to have his fun." Nico looked at his desk and fell quiet. He was beyond frustrated and on the brink of depression. Caroline was on his mind as much as the slayings. He had grown obsessed with the idea that she might leave him at a moment's notice, or that she had some bad news that threatened their future together. Tanya hadn't eased his mind, and he still hadn't talked with Caroline.

"Still nothing on Kevin Longin's mystery friend?"

"Nada."

"It's as if he never existed. What about our Wilde?"

"I've sent officers back to Eva Keller's apartment to look for the memory card with the documentary on it."

"And Noë Valles?"

"Plassard was able to come up with a man he followed from the Montparnasse station. He doesn't look at all like Etienne Delamare, but I've sent some detectives back with Etienne's picture. In either case—the law student and Valles's trick—both were young men between twenty and thirty years old."

"Etienne Delamare fits the age bracket."

"Yes, he's well-built and could easily appear older than twenty." Nico sighed.

"You're still upset about Caroline."

"Yes, Alexandre. I don't know what's bothering her."

"Why don't you ask her? That would be the easiest thing to do. I've never seen you like this, Nico, even when your mother was sick. You're falling apart."

Nico crossed his arms and looked out his window at the Seine and the Pont Neuf. He had spent so much of his life right here, in this office, with his son the only reason to go home at night. He couldn't imagine going back to that life—without the woman he loved.

"Look at you! Your cop shrink would have a field day with you."

That managed to nudge Nico out of his funk. He grinned as he recalled how Dominique Kreiss's presence on the team had annoyed the judge at first. Becker had initially been full of disdain for her theories, and he undervalued criminal profiling in general. But Kreiss had prevailed, and now Becker was a fan. Imagine that.

"At least I got a smile out of you," Becker said. "You've been so glum. Please, please resolve whatever it is that's going on with Caroline."

"I promise."

"You don't need to be afraid. Good God, she adores you."

"But she doesn't even want me touching her anymore."

"And you have to be touching her every minute of the day and night? Everyone needs a break once in a while."

Nico laughed. "You could be onto something."

"Just go talk to her. You'll clear the air, and everything will get back to normal."

"If only . . ."

"Nico! Now it's the examining magistrate talking. Take care of this, and do it quickly. I don't want your personal life interfering with our investigation. Understood?"

"Okay, okay."

"And keep me in the loop. Let's focus on the investigation. We don't want the killer's list getting any longer. Every minute counts. Speaking of which, tell your team that they'll be putting in more overtime than usual."

"Already done. They're at the service of the republic until we catch the copycat."

◆　◆　◆

Just as Nico was getting ready to go home, Professor Vilars called. He hesitated, fearing the conversation would strip him of the strength he'd been gathering to talk to Caroline. But he finally answered.

"What can I do for you, Armelle?"

"Where do I even start?"

"That bad? If this is about the Bois de Vincennes, tell me about the second right hand."

"It belongs to Kevin Longin. DNA confirmed it."

Nico was doodling as she spoke. Maybe that was the killer's signature—always finding a way to link the murders.

"Do the other body parts belong to a single man?"

"I was able to put the body back together from the pieces found in the woods and at the hotel. However, I'm still waiting for DNA confirmation."

"What kind of weapon do you think he used?"

"A handsaw. Captain Vidal hit it on the nose."

"Have you done an insect analysis?"

"Ah, yes, those loyal lieutenants. Did you know that carrion insects have been linked to death from time immemorial?"

Nico set his pen down and leaned back in his chair.

"Are you referring to Beelzebub, the Devil himself?" The original name, Ba'al Zebub, was often interpreted as "lord of the flies," suggesting that the link between decomposition and necrophagous insects had been recognized for a long time.

"We also have the Mesopotamian clay tablets that mention green and blue flies. The ancient Egyptian *Book of the Dead* explains how to keep them away in the preservation of mummies."

"Well, flies aren't that hard to observe when a body decays."

"True, but humor me while I share another factoid: in thirteenth-century China, a murderer was nailed because of the flies attracted to the blood on his knife."

"Professor, how many hours have you been at work?"

"Too many, obviously."

"What did our modern-day flies tell you?"

"*Protophormia terraenovae*, of the *Calliphoridae* family, more commonly known as blowflies. These shiny blue-green flies are among the first squatters. They start colonizing the body just a few hours after death, laying white or yellow eggs that look like grains of rice—a female can lay as many as two hundred eggs at a time. Those are the white splotches Captains Vidal and Rodon found on the body parts. At an average ambient temperature of twenty-five degrees centigrade, the eggs take twelve to twenty-four hours to hatch. So I'd say the death occurred no more than twenty-four hours ago."

Nico was looking at the maps. The day before, Noë Valles had followed a client from the Montparnasse station to a hotel suite, where the killer had cut him to pieces and spread his remains in the Bois de Vincennes.

"The victim was about a meter seventy-five tall, judging from the size of his femur."

That would correspond with Noë Valles.

"He had a tattoo on his inner left ankle: a crocodile, done with an electric tattoo machine."

"That corresponds with Noë Valles's description. What about the bite on the neck?"

"A bite leaves a bruise when it occurs before death. In this case, there's deep tissue alteration with bleeding, bruising, and coagulation, an irrefutable sign that it occurred antemortem. But the biter didn't stop there. He ripped off tissue, leaving a deep wound."

"A sadistic bite."

"Violent and sexual in nature. I took pictures and casts of the wound and sent them to the forensics lab. Professor Queneau will have a digital analysis done for comparison in the event of an arrest."

"No DNA?" Nico asked.

"We weren't able to collect enough saliva for a quality DNA identification."

"So no luck?"

"That's right. But the biter appears to have hypodontia."

"Which means?"

"Some of his permanent teeth never grew in. He's missing his upper canines. The most commonly missing teeth in Europeans are the third molar, followed by the mandibular second premolar, the maxillary lateral incisor, and the premolar. One in eighteen Europeans have this condition, but the absence of canines is rare."

"What can explain the condition?"

"Hypodontia can be caused by environmental factors, such as an infection or trauma, but usually it's genetic."

"Thanks. This could help."

"Let me know if you need anything else. I'm on call."

She didn't have to tell him what she was thinking. He knew. He could hear in her voice that she was worried about a fifth victim. Nico ended the call and held back an angry urge to knock everything off his desk. He felt powerless. Despite all their best efforts, the copycat was slipping through their fingers. Just as Caroline was slipping from his arms. What could she be so afraid of?

Nico opened his son's door.

"I saw your light on. You're not asleep yet? You have school tomorrow."

"Papa," Dimitri said, setting down his tablet. "I wanted to wait up for you."

Nico saw his son's gaze drop to the SIG Sauer in his holster. He had been so distracted, he had forgotten to remove the gun and put it in the safe. A mistake. Dimitri already had it in his head that his father might not come home one night. Was that why he was waiting up for him tonight?

"You know that as chief, I have an invisible shield that protects me, paid for by the department—"

"Dad, I'm fourteen years old. And you've already been shot once."

"But look at me now, all hale and hearty. They gave me that shield when I went back to work."

"Yeah, and I still believe in Spider-Man. You look tired. Go get some sleep."

"Good night, son."

"Good night . . . Hey, Dad, is something wrong with Caroline?"

"Why do you ask?"

"I don't know. She's been giving me kind of strange looks. And she seems sad. It's nothing serious, is it?"

Nico heard the anxiety in his voice.

"There's nothing to worry about. I'll investigate and solve the mystery."

Dimitri smiled and turned out his bedside lamp. He didn't believe in Spider-Man or Santa Claus anymore, and he was getting hair on his chest, but he was still a child.

Nico went into his room and locked up his service weapon. He heard the water running in the bathroom. Caroline was in the shower. He took off his clothes and stepped in with her. Soapy water ran between her breasts and down her belly. She was beautiful. Desirable.

"Holster your weapon, Inspector," she murmured.

He couldn't tell if she was being playful or not. He pulled her close, kissing her warm neck, stroking her slick hair, and letting go of everything but her. He ran his hands down her back and buttocks. She tensed up, but he wanted her so much. Now she was trembling. Nico pushed her up against the cold tiles, lifting her.

"No . . . Please. No . . ."

The words assaulted him like icy pellets. He set her down and just looked at her. Caroline started crying and crumpled in his arms.

He didn't know what to do. He felt like a confused teenager. Before he could figure it out, his phone rang. He pulled away and went to answer it. The prospect of the copycat spilling more blood was nowhere near as terrifying as the anguish Caroline was feeling.

"It's Théron, Chief."

"What did you find?"

"Fifty or so numbered memory cards buried under a fake plant. Who would have thought to look there?"

"You did. Good work, as usual."

"Eva's bookshelves were full of Arsène Lupin and Sherlock Holmes. She apparently loved a good mystery."

"Maybe that's why she wanted to do a documentary on serial killers."

"We're staying to watch the recordings, Chief. We'll keep you posted."

Nico clicked off. Caroline had crawled under the covers and curled into a fetal position, her back to him. Nico sat down next to her and put a hand on her shoulder.

"What is it, darling? Please, talk to me."

"It's nothing. I'll be fine tomorrow."

"Something has been bothering you, and I want to know what it is."

"You've got that investigation you're working on. I'm fine, really."

"Yes, I've got that investigation, but I'm worried about you."

She didn't say anything.

"Is it your work at the hospital?"

"No, Nico. Everything's fine at the hospital."

"Did I do something wrong?"

"No, I'm telling you! It's not you."

"Dimitri, then?"

"No. It's nobody else. It's me."

Caroline's shoulder was shaking. She was silently weeping. Nico wanted to take her in his arms and make the sadness disappear, but he knew she'd just push him away again. Nico studied her still-damp hair and her thin arm clutching the pillow, and he felt a nausea so intense, he almost had to run to the bathroom. How much more of this could he bear? Everything was spinning out of control, and there was nothing he could do about any of it.

20

Wednesday, May 15

Théron showed up in Nico's office brandishing a memory card.

"That woman was crazy about making films. She was Keller's daughter, that's for sure."

Nico called his secretary. "Round up Rost, Kriven, and Maurin, would you? And Kreiss, too. We've got a movie to watch."

He plugged the projector cable into his computer and inserted the memory card. He was just calling Deputy Commissioner Cohen when Judge Becker walked in, looking the worse for wear.

"I had a nightmare about Dorian Gray," Becker said, rubbing his face. "He was our copycat, and we were doing everything we could to nail him, but it was impossible to see his features."

Kriven had walked in. "So, our favorite judge is a psychic now," he said, grinning.

Deputy Chief Rost followed on his heels, with Commander Maurin and Dominique Kreiss not far behind. Cohen was the last to arrive. He smelled like cigar smoke, and Nico suppressed a smile. Old habits died hard. He doubted that the man would ever quit.

Nico hit "Play," and Mick Jagger's voice filled the office. *Serial Killers On-Screen* scrolled up, with blood dripping from the letters, like the opening of a bad horror movie.

Jagger was singing "God Gave Me Everything." Nico thought she would have chosen "Sympathy for the Devil," but then he heard the closing words: "I can't stop. I can't stop. I can't stop. I can't stop."

"Her boyfriend's idea?" Cohen had gotten out of his chair and was now pacing.

A young woman's voice replaced Jagger's, and then Eva appeared on the screen.

"Movies about serial killers have been around for more than seventy years. The first was Alfred Hitchcock's *Shadow of a Doubt*, and hundreds of serial-killer movies—both feature films and documentaries—have been made since then. They all reflect a cultural infatuation with these killers, who murder time and again for reasons only they know. The serial killer most depicted in film is, without a doubt, Jack the Ripper—perhaps because of the sheer violence and notoriety of his murders. But, as we've said, many other serial killers have inspired filmmakers. Here, we will look more closely at some of those movies. It's hard to think of a more compelling—or should we say gripping?—subject."

"Who's filming?" Théron asked. "One of the two kids we interviewed?"

Eva continued, "The first film is *Evilenko*, a 2004 English-language thriller. It flopped at the box office, but Malcolm McDowell turned in a masterful interpretation of Andrej Romanovich Evilenko's pedophilia and murderous urges, and David Grieco's production was very sophisticated. The story was loosely based on the Soviet serial killer Andrei Chikatilo."

"Well shit, there we have it!" Cohen shouted.

"'There is no happiness without tears, no life without death. Beware, I'm going to make you cry.' Those are the words of Lucian

Staniak, a Polish serial killer who did his dirty work in the 1960s. This warning raises questions. Who's better poised to lead us through the intricacies of suffering and despair than a serial killer?"

The screen filled with black-and-white stills of crime scenes.

"Let's fast-forward and see if Eva's list corresponds with the copycat's," Nico said.

He double-timed through the film's dark content, slowing down as Eva covered Thomas Quick and Fritz Haarmann. When there were just a few minutes left, he stopped.

"But the makers of feature films and documentaries aren't the only ones who've been inspired by serial killers. The creators of the Clock Tower horror games were as well. Clock Tower 3 references crimes committed by John George Haigh, the Acid Bath Murderer, who dissolved his victims in sulfuric acid."

The documentary stopped abruptly.

"I'd say the copycat wanted us to find this," Théron said.

"He's taunting us—making it clear that he's the gamemaster," Nico said. "We need to get out ahead of this."

"For now, he's still one step ahead," Becker said.

"I'll fill in Commissioner Monthalet," Cohen said. "I don't want anything about this documentary getting out. Nothing, do you understand? The reporters still think they're covering unrelated murders. If they get wind of a serial killer, the whole thing will go viral. It's complicated enough already. Now get to work. The killer has a leg up on us. Our job is to trip him up—before we find the fifth victim in an acid bath."

The deputy commissioner locked eyes with Nico, sending him a clear message. He needed to solve this case now. Cohen then turned on his heels and left.

"Maurin, get us everything you can on this John Haigh," Nico ordered. "Send someone to the Paris Bar Association with Etienne

Delamare's picture. Théron, find out more about that conference Eva attended."

Nico turned to Becker. "Alexandre?"

"Yes?"

"I think it's time to visit Etienne Delamare's home and do a little search of his place. Do you agree?"

"I'd say it's a good idea."

"Kriven, I'd like you to handle that. Remember, we're looking for a man, age twenty to thirty, right-handed, who wears a size 44 shoe. He's missing his upper canine teeth, lives in Paris, and is familiar with Louviers. We don't know if Etienne Delamare, the law student Eva Keller dated, and the man who picked up Noë Valles are similar in any way, but we need to find out. I want more information on them. Get everything you can, and keep in mind that he may be using disguises. Rost, I want you to supervise all this."

"Got it."

Nico was in high gear again.

"Ms. Kreiss, do you have anything to add?"

"Chikatilo, Thomas Quick, the Red Spider, Fritz Haarmann, and now the Acid Bath Murderer . . . The media played up all these killers, based on their signatures. As for our copycat, he's not only imitating his famous predecessors and revisiting European criminal history, but also leaving clues that allow us to link the murders. He doesn't want us giving credit for these slayings to anyone else. He wants all the glory. That's his signature. He's hungry for recognition and power. In addition, he's methodical, smart, and meticulous. And he wants us to know it."

"Then why hasn't he given the media a heads-up?" Kriven asked.

"Because he's only interested in the opinions of those in authority. That doesn't mean he won't promote his crimes to a wider audience when the time comes. Who knows. He may even create a fan club."

"Conclusion: pride is eating him up inside," Kriven said. Nico noted that he hadn't taken his eyes off the psychologist. Kreiss nodded, the hint of a smile on her lips.

"To your stations," Nico cut in. "David, I'm riding along."

Nico had set aside his worries about Caroline and was moving again. He was pumped.

"I'm in, too," Becker said.

Louis checked his backpack. He had an Enfield .38 revolver, a white envelope with four bullets symbolizing the lemon-yellow airplanes, rubber gloves, a gas mask, and an apron. Perfect. He also had three packets of concentrated sulfuric acid that he'd purchased online. He shivered at the thought of subjecting his prey to the details of his plan. There would be no resistance and very little apprehension. Perhaps even some excitement. There was no refusing a little tryst, and Louis had all the attributes necessary for seduction. The minx would get her due, on her knees, her eyes closed. He would be the master.

"John George Haigh was an English serial killer and a dandy. He murdered three men and three women between 1944 and 1949. He murdered for profit, using forgery to seize his victims' property after they were gone."

Captain Noumen had done his homework.

"He was arrested in March 1949 and hanged in August. Madame Tussaud's waxworks made a death mask of him. He left his clothes to the museum and stipulated that he should be kept spotless, with his pants neatly creased, his shirt cuffs exposed, and his hair neatly parted.

He wanted to be remembered for his elegance, even if it was in the Chamber of Horrors."

"Listen to this," Maurin said. "'I got a mug and took some blood, from his neck . . . and drank it.' He was a vampire."

"Gross."

"After consuming his victim's blood, he'd put the body in a metal drum and fill it with sulfuric acid. He'd drink tea while he waited for the acid to do its thing. After his arrest there was speculation that he was simulating mental illness to avoid the death penalty, but it didn't work. He was hanged in Wandsworth Prison. Ironically, he didn't have to simulate mental illness. He was downright psychotic—entirely egocentric and totally devoid of any feelings of guilt."

"It must be no different with our copycat," Maurin said.

"He did make mistakes, though," Noumen noted. "He thought the acid would destroy everything, but it didn't. In the case of one of the victims, police discovered gallstones, part of a left foot, pelvic and spinal bones, the acrylic resin used for dentures, the handle of a handbag, and a tube of lipstick in Haigh's rented workshop. They also found fatty traces inside the metal drums."

Maurin gagged.

"If Haigh's our copycat's teacher," Noumen said, "the student may have surpassed the teacher."

Commander Théron and his team walked through the gates of La Fémis. According to its brochure, the school was one of the world's most prestigious film academies. It was well situated in Montmartre. The neighborhood could have been a movie set.

The detectives crossed the narrow courtyard and stopped in front of the main office. This was where Marcel Carné shot *Les enfants du paradis* and Jean Cocteau made *Les parents terribles*. Théron walked up the steps. The school had certainly taught some future greats.

Théron showed his badge and asked to speak to the head administrator of the school. Flashing his badge always yielded the desired result. Two minutes later, a man with graying hair was shaking their hands. Théron ordered his team to canvass the school and followed the administrator into his office.

"Nobody told me you were coming," the administrator said, gesturing to a chair.

"We're conducting a criminal investigation. My team needs to talk to Eva Keller's classmates, show them a picture of a suspect, and try to come up with a portrait of a law student she met at a conference. I'd like to discuss this conference with you. There's no reason for alarm, I assure you."

"Eva's death has shocked all of us."

Just outside the man's door Théron could see students laughing in the hallway. "I'm sure," he said.

"What conference would you like to discuss?"

"A conference called 'The Abuse of Truth.' It took place sometime before Christmas and looked at serial killers as an inspiration for apprentice directors."

"What are you imagining? That one of them turned into a murderer after the conference? That's a bit of a stretch, don't you think?"

"Sometimes reality is stranger than fiction."

"I'll call in the person who organized the event," the chief administrator said, picking up his phone.

"She's already on her way."

The administrator's face was drawn. He clearly didn't want the school involved any more than it already was. Even after spending his whole life behind a camera, he had never envisioned this scenario.

◆ ◆ ◆

Rue des Jeûneurs had been all over the news a few weeks earlier, when the cops had cleared out a problematic squat in the area. Today, they were there for an entirely different reason. They entered a building next to a closed massage parlor. Two officers took up position in front of the door, while the others, with Nico, Kriven, and Becker in the lead, climbed the stairs to the top floor. They heard music playing inside the apartment. Kriven knocked on Etienne Delamare's door. The music stopped, and the door opened.

"Etienne Delamare?" Commander Kriven asked.

"Yes, what can I do for you?"

"Criminal Investigation Division. We'd like to talk to you."

"About what?" the young man said. He was a good meter eighty-five in height and had eyes the gray-green color of a pond.

"About your cousin Juliette," Nico said.

"I already told the police everything I know."

Becker stepped forward. "My name is Alexandre Becker. I'm the magistrate in charge of this case. Let us in. We have new information that we need to discuss with you."

Etienne looked disconcerted. He stepped aside. "Does my family know?"

Nico ignored the question. "I'm Chief Sirsky, and these are the other members of my team."

Captain Vidal distributed latex gloves, and the men spread out in silence.

"What are you doing?"

"We're exploring new leads in the investigation of Juliette's homicide," Nico answered, examining the spines of the books on the shelves.

"What does that have to do with me?"

"You are part of the family, and you split your time between Louviers and Paris. We have reason to believe that your cousin's murderer has committed crimes in the capital."

Nico had thrown a stone into the murky water, and now he'd watch the ripples.

"What? Are you saying that Juliette wasn't his only victim?"

"That's what we think."

"I still don't see what that has to do with me."

"A bedroom and a living room with a kitchen, plus a bathroom," Kriven said. "He lives alone. No sign of a roommate."

Nico took his eyes off the suspect and scanned the room, taking in a giclée print of a still life with interesting light and shadows.

"We must check out all possible leads," Becker said.

"Did you know Eva Keller, a student at La Fémis?" Nico asked, giving Etienne his full attention.

"The director's daughter? The one everyone's talking about? The girl who was murdered?"

"Yes," Becker said. His tone was sharp.

"No, I never met her."

"Did you attend a conference called 'The Abuse of Truth'?"

"Um . . . No."

"We'll have the list of participants soon, and we'll be able to check."

"You're treating me like I did something wrong. I loved Juliette like a sister."

"Do the names Kevin Longin or Noë Valles mean anything to you?"

"Nothing at all."

"Were you invited to an event at the Paris Bar Association?"

Etienne seemed genuinely surprised by the question.

"I wish, but I don't have those kinds of connections."

"Your aunt said that you changed your major to criminal law after Juliette was kidnapped."

"I told you. She was like a sister to me. So yes, I'd rather put killers behind bars than defend them—like you."

"Do you ever hang out near Montparnasse?" Becker asked.

"Trains to Normandy leave from the Saint Lazare station."

"Have you ever invited any of your friends from Paris to go with you?" Nico asked.

"Yes, but that was a long time ago."

"How long ago?"

"More than a year ago, after midterms."

"A friend who could have taken an interest in Juliette?"

"No! I don't think we even saw her."

"What was that friend's name?"

"It's someone I'm not even in touch with anymore."

Nico handed the young man a notebook. "Write down his name. Did you notice anything unusual when you last visited your family?" He noted that Etienne was right-handed.

"If you mean something that would explain what happened to Juliette, the answer is no—nothing."

"And otherwise?" Nico insisted.

Etienne bit his lip. *What is he thinking?* Nico wondered.

The Paris Bar Association served as a voice for some twenty thousand lawyers, defined ethics in the legal profession, and resolved conflicts. Chaired by a *bâtonnier*, it was run like a business, with a hundred and seventy employees and twenty-nine departments.

The ground floor of the Maison du Barreau, situated on a corner of Place Dauphine at the western end of Île de la Cité, had several elegant arches, while the upper floors featured a seventeenth-century-style brick exterior with multipane windows. The interior, however, was modern and functional. A receptionist ushered Commander Maurin and Captain Noumen upstairs to meet the bâtonnier's assistant.

"So, you want some details about the event we've planned for June?"

"I believe you've already sent out invitations," Maurin said.

"Not yet."

"But we found this."

The woman looked at the invitation discovered at the hotel.

"Who gave you that? It's not the right invitation, in any case." She sounded surprised.

"Do you know this man?" Noumen held out a photo of Etienne Delamare.

"No, I can't help you. However, some people who've been in the news lately did pay us a visit."

"Is that right," Maurin said, leaning forward in her chair. "And who would that be?"

The chief administrator of La Fémis pulled up the information on the conference. "About twenty of our students attended," he said.

"Can you print up the list, please?" Commander Théron asked.

"The conference was organized by students in the master's program at the Paris Criminology Institute. I won't be able to give you a complete list, as we only have the students from our school who attended."

The master's degree in criminology led to careers in the police and gendarmerie, as well as in prisons, customs, and the magistrature. Prospective lawyers also studied at the institute. Every year, some five hundred students applied for admittance, but only twenty-five were chosen. Around three hundred students attended each year.

Théron sighed. It was an elite place. Had a crack serial killer wormed his way in?

Ukraine, Sweden, Poland, Germany . . . Would the murderer emulate the British serial killer next? At first glance, it seemed to make sense.

But did it? Nico was trying to crawl into the brain of the copycat, but so much still didn't make sense.

He heard a knock at the door, and Deputy Chief Rost walked in.

"Eva Keller stopped by the Paris Bar Association two days before her murder to interview the bâtonnier for her documentary. Guess how she got the appointment? Through an old friend of the bâtonnier, Marianne Delvaux."

"The actress?"

"That's right, Chief. The woman who claimed she wasn't close to her lover's daughter was actually helping her with her homework. And she wanted us to believe that Eva knew nothing about the affair. She certainly deserves her César Award. By the way, the invitation to the Bar Association event is a fake. The association hasn't even sent them out yet. Did you get Maurin's memo?"

"About John Haigh? Yes."

"Enough to put the fear of God in us, right? So who do you think encouraged Eva Keller to change the subject of her documentary? Marianne Delvaux or the student she met at the conference?"

Nico was fit to be tied. The actress had tried to pull one over on them. "Bring Delvaux in. No more kid gloves for her. And I want to know who this Wilde is. He might be a criminology student. Do we have the complete list of those who attended the conference?"

"We're working on it, but it's long. And we're looking for Etienne Delamare's friend, the one who went to Normandy with him last year."

"The search of his apartment showed that he wears a size 44 shoe."

"And that he's right-handed. Kriven told me."

"Like 90 percent of the world's population. The search didn't turn up a freezer or any suspicious suitcases. We'll have to check his teeth."

"Kriven also said that Etienne walked in on the Bisots having a fight."

Nico nodded. "Apparently Mr. Bisot has a temper. He's told his wife to go to hell on more than one occasion. And Etienne is certain that his uncle's trips to Paris aren't just for work. He claims he has a mistress here. Etienne says the man isn't who he pretends to be, and Dr. Bisot is a basket case, not only because of her loss, but also because of the way he treats her."

"That doesn't make him a killer capable of murdering his own daughter," Rost said.

"True. But we need to keep in mind that the man we're after is a psychopath who wants everyone to think he's normal. Family gives a psychopath an aura of normalcy and respectability, something he would want to maintain—unless he's at the end of his rope and breaking down."

Nico folded his arms across his chest. "Did Kriven give you the other piece of news?" He didn't wait for an answer. "It seems Juliette wasn't Bisot's biological daughter. Her father died when she was one, and Mr. Bisot adopted her later. He has a son with Dr. Bisot. He could have considered Juliette an outsider in the family."

Nico watched Rost's face redden. "Damn it! Why are we only learning about this now? Why didn't that make it into the case file from the local police?"

"You know how it is when everyone knows everyone else. Lucky for us, Etienne leaked it at the end of our search. In any case, our copycat has committed a series of murders demonstrating real mastery and a genuine pleasure in killing. That's not a man at the end of his rope, a man lashing out at his loved ones, but we can't neglect any lead. Put a team on it."

Rost nodded and left the office. Nico watched him close the door and picked up his phone. He fiddled with it for a minute before making the call.

His mother picked up. "Nico?"

"Yes, it's me, Mom. How are you?"

He waited for Anya's answer.

"Is everything okay, son?" she finally said. He heard both worry and determination in her voice, and Nico knew that she wouldn't give up until she got answers. She could be worse than a detective.

"No, I'm not," he said, a knot in his throat.

"You can put on your 'everything's okay' act for everyone else, but I brought you into this world, remember? Of course you don't, but I do. My son, four kilos, two hundred grams. And you're still my baby. That's what being a mother is about."

Nico smiled. He hated to use the cliché, but she was the original drama queen.

"Now tell me what's wrong."

Anya never changed, thank God. She'd always have her way of cutting to the chase.

"The Keller case . . . and Caroline," Nico finally said, holding back his tears.

21

It was a perfect day for a stroll in the gardens of the Château de Versailles. She pulled on her gloves and checked the details of her costume, custom made at great expense by a seamstress who had supplied gowns for a historical-drama series on television. She loved these outings with this group of amateur actors who shared a passion for historical reenactments and a fascination for role-playing parties. Today she was playing Françoise-Athénaïs de Rochechouart, Marquise de Montespan.

After tying a final ribbon, she inhaled, her eyes closed, and enjoyed the fragrance of the freshly pruned bushes. She sensed instinctively that men were watching her. Why wouldn't they, with her honey-colored hair falling over her shoulders, her pearl-white skin glowing in the sunshine, and her hips swaying as she wandered along the walkway? Her looks were her greatest weapon, and she was skilled at brandishing them. Why wouldn't she? The world was a tough place, and she wasn't ashamed of using the means at her disposal.

"Madame Athénaïs?"

She recognized the man's voice and slipped into her role. He was waiting for her order. She nodded, and he tucked his instrument under his chin.

The man playing the king flashed her a hungry smile. But why had they chosen him to play the role? His nose wasn't long enough, and his eyes were all wrong. No matter. She wouldn't have to pretend with him today, as she was meeting someone else. She imagined stealing away to a discreet corner with him, feeling his caresses on her neck and his hand searching for her bosom. A wave of warmth spread across her belly. She loved the pleasures of the flesh, but even more than that, she loved the desire she stoked in her lovers. It made her feel powerful.

Everyone spread out in the garden, while the musician played the first notes on the violin.

"You are radiant, my dear!"

She turned and smiled at the woman playing Madame de Montespan's sister Gabrielle.

"I want to dance," Athénaïs said.

Gabrielle laughed.

"You always want to dance, especially when our Jean-Baptiste's playing the violin."

"Isn't he extraordinary?"

"Yes, he is. And you know how to bring out talent . . . like your beauty. These men have eyes only for you, and the women look at you with respect, fascination, and . . ."

"And what?"

"Jealousy."

"A dangerous emotion."

"For the one feeling it or for the recipient?"

Athénaïs made a face. She knew the risks of being the mistress of the king of France. She had to be on her guard at all times—especially when it came to slipping away and meeting a lover.

"Is everything all right?" Gabrielle asked. "We need to join the king. He won't start the promenade without you."

Her place was next to him. The Sun King's burning gaze made her uncomfortable, but she hurried over to him. She had a role to play.

"Ah, my dear!" said the king.

"I'm all yours."

"We were talking about our friend Molière, whom you hold in great esteem."

"A genius," she said.

The king nodded. "I agree."

As she smiled demurely and smoothed her gown, a valet slipped a note into her hand. What could it be?

"Is madame feeling well?" an attendant asked.

Athénaïs hadn't expected this twist in the role-playing game. She apologized to the king and slipped off to read the note. Had he changed his mind and decided against meeting her? She needed to find out. She sighed in relief when she read the message. He was waiting for her at the Colonnade—earlier than planned.

"I just couldn't wait any longer," he said when she reached him. "Forgive me."

"You want to leave now? We just got started."

"You can permit a slight breach, can't you?"

He was like a little boy who couldn't control his desires. She supposed it was normal at his age. Irritating at times, yes. But charming, too. He had so much to learn, and she so enjoyed teaching him.

"Let's go then," she said, as if she were granting him a favor.

"To your place?"

"Do you have a car? I came with someone."

"I do. Follow me."

He opened the passenger door for her, and once he slipped into traffic, he put a hand on her thigh.

"You'll have to hold on till we get to Rue Cambon," she whispered, feeling flattered by his impatience.

22

Nico's heart was racing as he entered Saint Antoine Hospital. Full of hope, he took the stairs two at a time and hurried into Dr. Caroline Dalry's department. He hadn't felt this nervous since he was a teen on a first date. Maybe, just maybe, she'd be happy to see him.

He glimpsed her in the hallway, dressed in her usual white coat, with four colored pens in her breast pocket. She didn't notice him until he got closer. When she did, the smile on her face disappeared, but he couldn't turn back now.

"What are you doing here?" she asked.

"I figured you might be missing me."

The doctor she'd been talking to gave Nico a nod and slipped away.

"Have you finished your rounds?" he asked.

"Nearly. I've got two more patients to see."

"I'll wait, and then you're coming with me."

"Where are we going?"

"Home," he said, hungry for her.

"You know everyone can see you," she teased.

Sometimes she acted like her usual self, but it never lasted long.

"Am I that transparent?"

She laughed. He hadn't heard her do that in days.

"Most definitely." She was still smiling.

"Shoot. I didn't do it on purpose, ma'am," he said, raising his hands. "It's entirely your fault."

"Is that so?"

"You're provocative, doctor."

"You'd say that even if I were wearing one of your old robes and a thick pair of wool socks."

"You have a point. That is, if you were naked under the old robe."

"Nico! You're obsessed."

"With you and only you, my sweet."

"Where's Dimitri?" she asked.

"He's spending the night with his grandmother."

"So you planned this all out," Caroline said, looking away.

"Finish up. I'm not going anywhere," he said, ignoring that she'd averted her gaze from him.

She kissed him on the cheek and turned around. Nico followed her with his eyes as she walked into a patient's room.

An hour later, Nico was pouring two glasses of Château-Chalon, a white wine from the Jura region, which he had tasted with his brother-in-law a few years earlier. Caroline had put on a pair of jeans and a simple tank top. He lit a candle and hit "Play," and U2's "One"—the version with Mary J. Blige—came on. They had made unforgettable love to this music once. Tonight, though, he felt the tension in her shoulders when he pulled her close.

"This feels like a trap," Caroline said.

"I don't have any ulterior motives. I just wanted to be alone with you."

She smiled her magnificent smile, which always made his stomach flutter, and pushed aside her glass.

"I'm not really in the mood for a drink."

He said nothing and stood up. Taking her hands, he brought her to her feet. "How about a slow dance, then?"

"I'm really sorry," she said in barely a whisper.

He held her tight. He wouldn't let her go.

"I didn't want to . . . It's idiotic," she murmured.

It felt like the floor was falling out from under him. What was she trying to say?

"I'm so sorry, Nico. I'm a doctor, and I know about these things. I'm taking responsibility, and I messed up. I feel so stupid. I didn't mean . . ."

She was crying now, her tears wet on his cheeks. He held her close, still swaying to the music.

"If you want to be free again, I won't stop you. I'll understand," she said. "I won't ask anything of you."

He pulled back and gazed in her eyes.

"What are you talking about? Why would I ever want to be free again? What are you trying to tell me, Caroline?"

Her eyes were red, and she looked scared.

"Are you sick? Is that it? Don't you know by now that I'd never abandon you?"

"I'm pregnant."

Nico felt the blood drain from his face. Shocked, he let go of her. Caroline stared at him for a half second and then turned her back to him. She was going to leave—he knew it—but he quickly came to his senses. The voice in his head was shouting, "Do something, damn it! Now!" He grabbed her arm and pulled her close.

23

Thursday, May 16

A call straight from dispatch—that was a bad sign.

"Chief Sirsky?"

"Yes, it's me."

All calls for the police went through dispatch first. Then dispatch alerted the appropriate unit. Dispatch usually didn't call the chief directly.

"A maniac is holed up in an apartment on Rue Cambon. He called emergency services at 9:51 this morning to report a homicide. He asked to speak directly to the chief of the Criminal Investigation Division. He mentioned a body burned in a bathtub. He won't let anyone in."

Nico's gut cramped. A body burned in a bathtub. He looked at his watch: it was 10:45.

"Do we know who the man is?"

"He won't say."

"Who lives in the apartment?"

"Virginie Ravault, a lawyer. Divorced, with two children."

"Is she the victim?"

"The man won't say. He's totally incoherent."

"And the children?"

"At school. We checked."

"Good. I'll take over from here."

Nico alerted Kriven's squad, and they responded as though their own lives depended on it. Wound as tight as a spring, Kriven led them into Nico's office. Vidal was complaining, as usual, but that was who he was. Plassard threw out a crude joke. They all laughed before turning their attention to what awaited them on Rue Cambon. For the first time in a long while, Nico felt indestructible, thanks to Caroline. He had that invisible shield, after all.

Local precinct officers had already arrived at Rue Cambon, a narrow one-way street in a fancy part of town near the Tuileries Gardens, and cordoned it off.

"Mrs. Ravault lives on the top floor," an officer told Nico. "You can see her apartment from here. The balcony with the flowers is hers."

The special interventions unit had arrived and taken up positions at strategic points. These masked officers were cold-blooded ninjas—their slogan: "Serve without fail."

Onlookers armed with cell-phone cameras lurked behind the police cordon waiting for something to happen.

"We've sighted him," said the head of the special interventions unit. "He appears to be alone."

"Is he armed?" Nico asked.

"That's what he says. We haven't seen anything yet."

"I'm going up."

"Put on a vest, Chief."

He strapped on the vest without a word. He didn't care to explain that even without one, nothing could stop him now.

"We'll cover you," the ninja said.

"I'm going with him," Kriven said, grabbing another vest.

The ninja glared at him, spoke a few code words into his walkie-talkie, and escorted them to the elevator. He was clearly used to being in charge, but he would soon be disabused of that notion. When they reached the top floor, Nico brushed past him and took the lead.

"Chief Nico Sirsky here!" he shouted through Virginie Ravault's door.

He felt the masked men shift behind him. They were used to stealth. But there was no time for that.

"You asked for me, and I'm here."

"Are you alone?" asked the voice from the other side of the door.

"One of my men is with me."

"You're the one I want to talk to."

It sounded like a wish, not an order. The guy seemed more lost than dangerous.

"How about I come in with Commander Kriven? Two won't be too many. You say there's been a murder?"

"It's true. My God . . . What happened here?"

He sounded like a frightened child. The ninjas could go home.

"Open up, and tell us what's going on."

"I saw you on TV!" the man yelled. "They said you handle major crimes, and you're a super cop."

People shouldn't believe everything they saw on television.

"I want the best person for this!"

"For what?"

"For . . . Virginie."

"Who is she to you?"

"My ex-wife."

Apparently, he was still in love with her.

"I took the kids to the movies yesterday afternoon. She had something to do and needed a hand. I brought them back at the end of the day, but when I rang the bell she didn't come to the door. So I took them home with me for the night. I dropped the kids off at school this morning, and then I tried to call her. She wasn't home, and she wasn't at her office, either. Everyone there was worried, because she had missed her first appointments of the day. You don't know my wife. Her job is very important to her. By this time I was really worried, so I came here and used my key to get in."

Nico heard a tinge of guilt in his voice. Maybe she didn't know he still had a key.

"And I found her! Shit! Fucking shit! I found her. And now I can't leave her. Do you understand?"

He was whimpering.

"Where is she?"

"In the bathroom."

"You should let me in, Mr. . . . . Ravault?"

"Yes, she kept my name. It was what she always used for work. And she wanted to have the same name as the kids."

Maybe, to him, it meant that they weren't entirely finished. *If you're that much in love,* Nico thought, *you'll hang on to any remnant of hope.*

"You're right," Nico said. "Having the same name is better for the children. Can you open the door now? I want to help you, but I can't do anything for you if I'm in the hallway."

They heard the lock turning. Head ninja assumed a combat pose.

"Don't try anything," Nico ordered. "I got this."

Their guard stood down. The situation was no longer his responsibility. The door opened, and a shadow of a man stood before them. He was disheveled and distraught, his face swollen from crying. Nico figured he probably couldn't even remember his children's names. He entered the apartment, with Kriven on his heels. The place was luxurious and bathed in light.

"The bathroom . . ."

The man showed them the way. Nico gently pushed the door open, and a vision more horrifying than his worst nightmare assaulted him.

Third-degree burns, acid eating away at the flesh. Her body, immersed in a brown bath, was unrecognizable.

"Did you touch anything?" Nico asked in a low voice.

"No. There's more over there." Mr. Ravault pointed to a corner.

Nico followed his finger. A note above the body; a rubber apron, gloves, and a gas mask lay on the floor. It was then that something else assaulted him: the vile odor. But inhaling sulfur wasn't just unpleasant. It was dangerous. Breathing it could cause chest pain, dizziness, low blood pressure, and a rapid pulse, as well as respiratory problems. Nico was already suffocating. He pushed Mr. Ravault and Kriven out of the room and shut the door. Mr. Ravault was coughing.

"Call the paramedics," Nico ordered. "Mr. Ravault needs oxygen. And tell Vidal he'll need some equipment."

Then he prayed that Virginie Ravault had experienced the same destiny as John Haigh's victims, all of whom had been shot in the head before being plunged in acid.

Finally, he reflected on the handwritten message taped above the bathtub: "Still life with lemons."

When the rescue squad arrived, they had Mr. Ravault take off his contaminated clothing. They rinsed his eyes and gave him oxygen. Meanwhile, Nico and Kriven waited for Vidal to arrive with protective filters, glasses, gloves, and bodysuits.

"We're taking him to the hospital," one of the paramedics told Nico. "There's a risk of a pulmonary edema. And that bathtub should be pumped as soon as possible. Sulfuric acid is extremely dangerous and reacts violently with water."

"I imagine the worst is past," Nico said.

"The bathwater must have boiled as soon as it mixed with the acid," the paramedic said. "It was probably some time ago."

When Vidal arrived with the necessary equipment, they geared up and went in.

Almeida was the first to say anything. "A piece of fried meat."

Nico, knowing full well that he was distancing himself from his feelings, didn't reprimand him.

"Let's just hope he killed her first," Vidal said. He delicately pivoted her head. "There's a bullet wound in the back of the skull. But I can't tell if it was inflicted before or after she died."

"The killer is taking more liberties and diverging from his models," Nico said. "None of John Haigh's victims were found in bathtubs. He used metal barrels."

"The exit wound is in the left temple," Vidal said.

"No trace of impact on the wall," Almeida said.

"Check the other rooms," Nico said. *"Still Life with Lemons on a Plate,"* he mused. "Van Gogh. I saw a reproduction of that painting just yesterday."

"A .38!" Kriven shouted. "In the bedroom."

"Haigh shot with an Enfield .38, which he kept in a hatbox," Nico said.

"This is an Enfield, too," Kriven called out. "Along with an envelope containing four bullets. I believe we've got our 'four planes a pretty lemon yellow.'"

"I'm going to look around the apartment," Nico said as Vidal carefully removed what was left of the body from the bathtub.

"Fancy lingerie, sex toys . . . Mrs. Ravault took her pleasures seriously," Kriven said. "But look at that piece of clothing on the carpet over there."

Nico picked up what looked like an elaborate seventeenth-century gown.

"I'm guessing it's a costume of some sort—a very expensive costume. We'll have to ask Mr. Ravault. Maybe he has some idea why she had this."

Nico moved into the living room and continued his silent examination for several minutes until he stopped in the middle of a wall.

"Take a look at this," Nico said, motioning to Kriven and then pointing to a painting. "There was another painting on this wall before that was bigger. The space all around this painting is lighter than the rest of the wall."

"Guys, see if you can find the painting that was here!" Kriven called out.

Nico took the painting down and read the title on the back. "*View of Santander* by Joris Hoefnagel. Looks Flemish."

"Santander—it's an old Spanish port city," Kriven said.

"The bigger painting is in the office," Almeida called from the other room. "It's a Bernard Buffet—an original. Undressed women."

"That seems more like her style," Kriven said. "She doesn't strike me as the kind of woman who'd switch a Buffet original for a cheap reproduction of an old port town."

Nico turned to Kriven. "Go ask Almeida if Santander means anything to him."

Nico didn't think this was some whimsical move. Virginie Ravault was clearly an orderly and meticulous woman. He could have eaten off her floor. The woman's tastes ran to things sensual and expensive, and she had the means to satisfy her appetite.

Kriven came back into the living room. "Santander's in Cantabria, in northern Spain. There's a beach close to it called El Sardinero with waves high enough to surf. Almeida's been there."

"Virginie Ravault and Spain—what's the connection? Ask Rost to look into it. Look for what doesn't belong."

"Exactly. Just like Van Gogh's painting *Still Life with Lemons*. Does it ring any bells?"

Kriven frowned.

"There was a reproduction at Etienne Delamare's place. The sun was lighting up the lemons like lightbulbs."

Kriven whistled. Then he grabbed his phone, which was buzzing, and Nico heard him talking to Rost.

"He wanted me to tell you that he's meeting Marianne Delvaux at headquarters this afternoon, and Juliette Bisot's father is coming in first thing tomorrow morning," Kriven said.

"Perfect. You can finish up here. I'm going to go have a talk with Etienne Delamare. He needs to explain his *Still Life with Lemons*."

Nico met Becker on the Boulevard Saint-Michel, near the Latin Quarter and the Rue Mouffetard, where his paternal grandparents had once owned a shop. They were Polish Roman Catholics who attended Saint Médard Church. Anya, on the other hand, had been raised in the Orthodox tradition.

"Is he in class?" Becker asked, without so much as saying hello.

"In a lecture. I wasn't keen on the idea of calling in backup and storming the place."

"But the kid may be a serial murderer."

"Yes, but a more subtle approach will work just as well. I'll go in, push my way past a few students, and sit down next to Etienne. Then I'll flash him a sharkish grin."

"He'll fall apart in his seat."

"Poor fellow."

The two men entered the Panthéon-Assas University.

"You may go through the main door when you arrive on time, and the side door when you're late," a secretary said.

Nico nearly laughed and headed straight for the main entrance of the fifteen-hundred-seat amphitheater. He searched for Etienne, a task that proved easier than expected as the room was far from full. Becker stopped in the center aisle and stood impassively at the end of the row while Nico made his way toward the young man. Down below, standing behind a desk and a microphone, the professor rambled on. He hadn't noticed their arrival.

Nico made it clear to Etienne's neighbor that he needed to move down a seat, and he settled down, smiling like a carnivore.

Etienne swallowed hard. "Wh-what are you doing here?" he stammered.

"I have a few questions. About Vincent Van Gogh."

"Excuse me?"

"I understand you're a Van Gogh specialist. In fact, you're the go-to guy on the subject, isn't that right?"

Etienne moistened his dry lips. His hand was shaking.

"You should gather your things and follow me. This is not the right place to talk about art."

"But my class . . . I have an exam soon and . . ."

Nico leaned over.

"And I'm looking for Juliette's murderer," he whispered in the boy's ear.

Etienne stood up, ready to do what Nico asked.

"It appears that some of my students think they already know everything," the professor said, staring at them. "I wonder whether they really believe they can pass the exam without attending my class."

Nico smiled at the professor and closed the lecture-room door behind them.

"We could take you to headquarters, but I don't want to waste any time," he said.

"What about the Luxembourg Gardens?" Becker suggested. "There are some out-of-the-way benches there."

"Sounds good," Nico said, grabbing Etienne's arm and hustling him down Rue d'Assas into the gardens. A few minutes later, they were seated on a secluded bench.

Nico sighed. "So, Van Gogh . . ."

He and Becker were sitting on either side of Etienne, their thighs nearly touching his.

"Vincent Van Gogh was a prolific creator of still lifes," Becker said. "He used them to experiment with colors and techniques, especially after his move from the Netherlands in the late 1800s. It was here in Paris that his approach became more expressive." He'd obviously done his homework. "Personally, I prefer *The Starry Night*, but that's a matter of taste."

Etienne Delamare didn't say anything, but both of his hands were shaking now.

Nico took over. "Clearly, you like lemons."

"I don't understand," Etienne murmured, his voice hoarse. "Please, I don't understand."

Nico looked at him without saying a word. The boy was a good actor.

"*Still Life with Lemons*," Nico finally said. "Does that mean anything to you? There's a reproduction of it at your place."

"That's why you—"

"Where did it come from?" Nico asked, cutting him off.

"It was a gift."

A mother and a toddler were walking past them. The youngster was so wobbly, it looked like she had taken her first steps only a few days earlier. She was grinning, clearly pleased with herself, and her mother was watching every step. Then, in the blink of an eye, she tripped and fell. Before she could even squeal, her mother swooped down and picked her up.

"There you go," the mother said, kissing the little girl and putting her back on her feet. The toddler was smiling again, and off they went.

"Who gave it to you?"

"A friend, as a thank-you."

"What friend? As a thank-you for what?"

"For . . . for inviting him to my place."

Etienne seemed completely disoriented.

"Inviting him over for dinner?"

"No . . . to Louviers."

"To your parents' place in Louviers? Is he the student you mentioned before? The one from last year?"

Etienne nodded. His eyes were wide, and he was shaking all over. Farther down the tree-lined path, an old woman was tossing bread crumbs to the pigeons.

"His name is Lucas Barel. He's studying law, too."

"Is he in the lecture room now?"

"I didn't see him."

"That's an odd gift, don't you think?" Becker said.

"That's what I thought, but since he used to come over to the apartment a lot, I didn't want to offend him."

A little boy ran past them, a toy sailboat in his hand. When Nico was a child, he had pushed his own toy sailboat around the park's Grand Bassin pond. Nico had brought Dimitri here when he was six or seven. Would Dimitri's little brother or sister have a toy sailboat someday, too?

Nico suppressed a smile and turned back to Etienne. "When was the last time Lucas Barel was at your place?"

"My answer is the same as it was yesterday: we don't see each other anymore."

"So why didn't you take down the Van Gogh?"

"It's become part of the décor."

"How did such a fine friendship come to an end so suddenly?"

"No special reason. Time goes by, and people change."

"Him or you?"

"Him or me what?"

"Which of you changed?" Becker asked.

"Both of us, probably. He was always hanging around, and it was starting to get on my nerves."

"In what way?"

"I don't know. He was just weird."

"Did Lucas Barel ever come on to you?" Nico asked, lowering his voice.

Etienne Delamare blushed.

"That's it, isn't it."

"That's what it seemed like."

"Do you know a lawyer by the name of Virginie Ravault?"

"No, not at all."

"Ravault, a criminal lawyer," Becker said.

"No, I'm sorry."

Nico figured they had gotten as much information as they were going to. He gave Becker a nod.

"You are not to leave Paris," the judge said.

"You mean I can't go home to Louviers?"

Nico glanced at Becker and looked back at the boy. "That's the only place you're allowed to travel to. Understand?"

"Yes, sir."

They stood up, and the boy followed suit.

"You're free to go, but remember what we've told you," Becker said, his tone firm.

Once they were out of earshot, Becker turned to Nico. "This *Still Life with Lemons* is really kind of astonishing, don't you think?" he asked.

Yes, it was astonishing. But for the first time, Nico was seeing beyond their investigation. He was going to be a dad again, and that was more mind-blowing than anything else.

24

You still have a little time to think it over, Caroline had texted him.

A little time before what? Before she ended the pregnancy? Before he told her he wasn't up for having another child, and she'd have to do it on her own? How could she even suggest such a thing? Hadn't she seen the happiness in his eyes? How could she doubt for a second the love he felt for her—and their child? He had held her tight after she broke the news. But he had been so overcome that he couldn't express exactly what he was feeling. His feelings were too big for words. There was no way he could summarize them in a text message.

Let me take you out for dinner tonight, he texted back. The whole world could go to hell tonight, but he wasn't going to hell with it.

He turned to Deputy Chief Rost and his three squad commanders. "What did you find out?"

Becker was giving him an odd look. The judge was clearly satisfied to see the warrior back at work, but the friend was wondering what was up.

"It's heavy stuff," Rost said. "You won't be disappointed. First . . . Santander."

He paused and repeated "Santander" softly for effect. It reminded Nico of the way Charles Foster Kane had murmured "Rosebud" on his deathbed in Orson Welles's film classic *Citizen Kane*.

Rost raised his voice again and continued, "In 1987 and 1988, at least sixteen women between the ages of sixty-one and ninety-three were raped and killed in and around Santander. The culprit: José Antonio Rodriguez Vega, a.k.a. the Old Lady Killer. He was born in Santander and began his criminal career when his mother kicked him out of the house after he had beaten up his terminally ill father. He was sent to prison on rape charges in 1978 but was released early for good behavior. It's believed that's when he began his homicidal spree. He was arrested again in May 1988 and sentenced to four hundred and forty years in prison. But he didn't last that long. Two inmates stabbed him to death in 2002."

Had something precious been taken away from José Antonio Rodriguez Vega, just as Charles Kane's parents had been ripped from him? Childhood traumas had a way of never healing.

"Vega was considered an honest and hard-working man," Rost said. "He would observe his prey from afar, use his charm to gain their trust, and get himself invited into their homes. Then he'd rape and suffocate them. Sometimes he'd also beat them."

Kriven was pacing. "How can we possibly guess who his next victim will be? It's impossible, because nothing links Juliette Bisot, Kevin Longin, Eva Keller, Noë Valles, and Virginie Ravault."

"Tell me about Mrs. Ravault," Nico said.

"She was a criminal lawyer in a high-profile firm. We'll be questioning her two associates, of course. She handled a few tough cases and knew some real bastards. Divorced, mother of two teenagers. She had a hobby—role playing—and she loved murder parties. She was part of a group that organized a reenactment yesterday afternoon at Versailles. That's why her ex was taking care of the kids, and it also explains the gown we found in her apartment. Mrs. Ravault was playing

Françoise-Athénaïs, Marquise de Montespan, a mistress of King Louis XIV, who, it was rumored, poisoned one of her rivals. The scene they were reenacting yesterday was a promenade."

"Contact the organizers," Becker said. "When did she leave? Was she alone? Why didn't she come to the door when her ex-husband tried to drop off the children or answer the phone when he called?"

"We're on it," Rost said. "But we've saved the best for last. Maurin, will you do us the honor?"

"Mrs. Ravault taught at the Criminology Institute, and she participated in that 'Abuse of Truth' conference."

"Well, shit!" Kriven blurted out.

"So we have a connection between Eva Keller and Mrs. Ravault: both of them were at the conference," Nico said. "Théron, did you dig up anything on Lucas Barel?"

"He's studying law with Etienne Delamare, as you know. He's the one who visited Etienne's family in Louviers last year. And guess what? He was also at the conference, even though it was primarily for students majoring in criminology."

"Bring him in," Nico ordered. "Let's find out if he's right-handed and wears a size 44 shoe. I want to know if he's our Oscar Wilde. Also, bring in the students who were working with Eva Keller on that project. They might be able to identify him. Let's see if he's missing his canines, too. Has Virginie Ravault's autopsy started?"

"A while ago. Vidal is there," Kriven said.

"Marianne Delvaux will be in soon," Rost said. "Who gets the honor of talking to her?"

"You and I will handle that—with a little less diplomacy than we used at Ladurée," Nico said.

"I can't wait."

"The head and upper third of the torso are relatively well preserved," Professor Vilars observed. "I imagine the victim was in a half-seated position. Do you see these burns on her lips and chin? There are some in her mouth, too. I can deduce that the attacker forced her to drink the poison, and she spit out the first mouthful. These lesions are antemortem. My examination of what remains of her air passages will confirm that."

"So he only shot her afterward," Vidal said. "He wanted her to know how she was going to die and what he would do to her remains."

"I believe that diverges from the Acid Bath Killer's modus operandi."

"Sick bastard! He deserves to fry in hell."

"Captain, it's not our job to pass judgment, so let's avoid that kind of comment here," the professor scolded.

"Still, I wouldn't mind hurrying along that trip to hell," Vidal said. He was pushing back, but oddly, the thought calmed him down.

Franck Plassard knew absolutely nothing about the world of role playing. The whole thing seemed frivolous. He had the real deal every day.

"In the seventeenth century, the Marquise de Sévigné hosted mystery parties," explained the director of the association that Mrs. Ravault belonged to. "The idea that the English came up with the idea is absolutely wrong. All that country did was revive the concept in the 1960s, which is when it also caught on in the United States."

Plassard almost rolled his eyes.

"I started participating in 1984, and we've had a good run, despite a suicide in the nineties. We have thousands of members."

"Including Mrs. Ravault."

"Yes . . . Virginie! She loved it. But why do you mention her in particular? Our association has so many members."

What did the man think? That he was here for a history lesson?

"Where were you yesterday?"

"I was with the players. The organizers always participate in the party, playing characters to help guide the game. The idea is to be interactive. It demands observation and creativity."

Plassard could tell the director wanted to keep going—and going. He stopped him. "How many participants were there?"

"About sixty."

"Tell me about them."

"Our membership fees are high, so most of them are well off. They tend to be professionals, upper management of large companies, business owners, and so on."

"Not everyone can be part of the Sun King's court, I suppose," Plassard said, feeling cheeky. "I'll need a complete list of the people who were involved yesterday."

"I'll print it out right away. Did something happen?" he asked, launching the printer.

"I'm afraid so."

"Is it serious?"

"Rather. What time did the party end?"

"Around ten. We went on a bit longer than usual."

"Did Mrs. Ravault stay until the end?"

"Actually, she didn't, and that was highly unusual. Our participants almost always do. We had to improvise because she left early."

Judging by the look on the director's face, Plassard gathered that the organizers liked only so much improvisation.

"Did she tell you she was leaving?"

"No, in fact, she didn't. A valet slipped her a message, and she vanished."

"A valet?"

"Someone playing the role of a valet. You know, like a butler."

"Right . . . And what did this message say?"

"The valet wasn't authorized to read Madame de Montespan's private correspondence, but you know how a king's staff can be . . ."

"Curious."

"Exactly. Well, someone was waiting to meet her. Some gentleman friend. And you know how women are . . ."

Plassard almost choked. This man was clueless.

"And who was this gentleman?"

"No idea. I don't even know if the message was real. It could have been a fake message from a rival who was eager to get rid of her and take her place beside the king. Many women were jealous of Madame de Montespan."

"And Mrs. Ravault?"

"Um . . . Virginie? We all like her. We've played together for years."

"Have you added any new members recently?"

The director's eyes lit up, and he leaned in.

"We get new members all the time, even people connected to show business. As a matter of fact, we just attracted the son of a celebrity. Michael Delvaux, Marianne Delvaux's son, has joined our group."

Kriven and Almeida walked into Mrs. Ravault's law firm to meet with her two associates, who appeared in well-tailored gray suits and blue shirts. They both had gray hair, and Kriven guessed they were in their early fifties.

"Virginie liked working on sensitive cases," one of them said. "Rapes, sexual abuse of minors, and blood crimes."

"Did she take an interest in her clients?" Kriven asked.

"Of course. Everyone deserves a defense. But as you can imagine, some clients are easier to like than others."

"You never refuse a client?"

"Yes, in fact, we do. Unless it's a charity case that really appeals to us, our clients must have the money to pay. And our caseload is occasionally so full that we can't take on anyone new."

"So did her clients like her?"

"For the most part," the other associate said. "But she had a strong personality and clashed with people every now and then."

"Oh?" Almeida said, keeping his tone impassive. "Did she ever get any threats?"

"Sometimes she got threatening letters, like we all do," the first associate said. "But she didn't let them affect her."

"But did any of the letters wind up getting to her? Did she receive any recently?"

The two men exchanged a glance.

"Yes to both of those questions," the first associate said. "Somebody was sending her a letter every month. They started coming five months ago, and they always arrived on the same day—the fifteenth."

Virginie Ravault had been murdered on the night of May 15.

"And yesterday as well?"

"Yes."

"Where are these letters?"

"In her office, I assume."

"Lieutenant Almeida will go get them. I'm sure a secretary can show him the way."

Almeida stood up.

"The first couple of months, we weren't terribly concerned. We thought it was just some crackpot. But when they kept coming, we wanted her to call the police. She refused. If only she had . . ."

"So the letters didn't scare her?" Kriven asked.

"She took them in stride at first—she thought her ex-husband might be behind them. But the last few letters seemed to get to her."

"Why would she think it was her ex-husband? Was he abusive?"

"Let's just say that he wouldn't let her go. But eventually she realized it wasn't him."

"How did she come to that conclusion?"

"She just knew. He was still in love with her, yes, but he wouldn't have stalked her."

"What about her clients? Could it have been someone who was angry over a conviction?"

"Anything's possible, but that kind of thing happens in the movies more than in real life."

"Did she tell you what the letters said?" Kriven asked.

"They always said the same thing: 'Arrogant bitch, I'm going to fuck you.'"

"A real poet." Kriven turned to the other lawyer. "She taught classes at the university, right?"

"At the Criminology Institute," the lawyer said.

"And she spoke at conferences?"

"She was a highly regarded criminal lawyer." The associate paused for a moment and cleared his throat. "Let's just say she liked sharing her experience."

"I'm getting the impression that it wasn't just professional experience that she shared. Am I right?"

The two lawyers looked at each other again.

"She enjoyed the company of young men," the second associate said. "You may find that useful in your investigation."

"Do you have any names?"

"None in particular."

"Lucas Barel? Etienne Delamare? Do either of those names mean anything to you?"

The two men shook their heads.

Almeida returned, the envelopes in hand. "I found them," he said.

Kriven took the envelopes and calmly opened the first one. The writing was angular and red. He looked up at Almeida and handed it over. "It's him."

Then he opened the rest. They were all the same. The copycat had planned everything well in advance. Even before Kevin, Eva, Noë, and little Juliette, Virginie Ravault was on his list.

Kriven turned to the lawyers. "Do you have any recollection of a student who might have stopped by here to see her? Or do you remember a particular argument with a client? Anything that could help us find out who wrote these letters?"

The first associate shook his head. "Nothing, really."

"Did you know that Mrs. Ravault enjoyed role-playing games?"

"Yes, she asked us to go with her once. She had an event yesterday at Versailles."

"Where were you then?"

"I was here, working," the first associate said.

"I was in court until late last night," the other replied. "Then I came back to the office and did some paperwork."

"When did you go home?"

The second associate sighed. "All right, detective. We know where you're going with this. We're criminal lawyers, after all. I went home around ten. My wife can confirm it."

"And I was doing paperwork with my secretary until eight," his colleague said. "After that, I had dinner at Lasserre."

A two-Michelin-star restaurant. That alibi would be easy to check.

"We'll come back later with an order allowing us to take Mrs. Ravault's professional engagement calendar and files," Almeida said.

"We're available if you need us."

"Perfect," Kriven concluded.

The second associate accompanied Kriven and Almeida to the door. But instead of saying good-bye, he followed them outside. Once he'd made sure the door was closed behind them, he took Kriven's elbow. "Virginie had a relationship with a young man who came here once. A . . . well . . ."

"Who was it?"

"The son of that actress Marianne Delvaux."

Lucas Barel lived on Rue de Javel, near the Félix Faure metro station in the fifteenth arrondissement. The street owed its name to a factory located here in the eighteenth century that manufactured a bleach called *eau de*

javel. After making sure all the exits were guarded, Commander Maurin and her team entered the building. Captain Noumen rang the bell when they reached Lucas's apartment. There was no answer so Maurin called out, ordering Barel to open up. A neighbor came out to the landing.

"He hangs out at Bistro 12, on the corner of Avenue Félix Faure. I heard him leave about a half hour ago."

"Thank you, sir."

"No problem. Nothing serious, I hope."

"We just have a few questions for him."

"That guy is creepy. I wouldn't be surprised if he was mixed up in something shady."

The man went back into his apartment, and the detectives dashed down the stairs, determined not to miss Lucas Barel.

With its red seats and plastic tabletops, Bistro 12 was a bar and brasserie much like others all over the capital. It served up sauerkraut, tripe, and steaks for lunch, as well as open-face sandwiches and salads for those watching their weight. Lucas Barel was seated at an outdoor table, drinking coffee and reading a law review. *Easy target,* Maurin thought. She nodded to the rest of her team, who discreetly stationed themselves around the area. He could run like a rabbit, but he'd have six armed hunters on his heels. She approached Barel, taking care to block the sun when he looked up.

"Lucas Barel?" she asked.

His eyes grew suspicious.

"Criminal Investigation Division. Please follow me. We have some questions for you."

"About what?"

"We'll talk at headquarters."

Noumen approached, his open jacket revealing his service weapon.

"Do not force me to be more specific, Mr. Barel."

"I have to study for my exams, so why don't you just tell me what you want right now? I'm sure we can settle this here."

Maurin put a hand on the grip of her holstered gun. "What you're going to settle is your bill. Then you're going to get up without causing a fuss, unless you'd rather be cuffed."

Barel swallowed hard and said nothing as they led him away. "But what is this about?" he finally asked once he was in the back of an unmarked car.

"It's about Vincent Van Gogh," Noumen said. "And the bitter taste of lemons."

Like most successful actresses in the movie industry, Marianne Delvaux was an attractive woman. Nico could only imagine how much effort it took her to stay that way as she approached fifty. Given that her face was as smooth as a baby's behind, she had undoubtedly been to a plastic surgeon many times.

"Please remove your sunglasses," Deputy Chief Rost asked politely.

They wanted to be able to read her eyes. But that might be more difficult with Delvaux than other suspects, since her eyes were capable of expressing anything she wanted. She was a professional.

"This is an interrogation," Rost said. "You will be recorded and filmed. It's standard procedure."

"I'm aware of that. I've been in cop shows before. But I don't know what you want from me. I already told you about William and his daughter. I'm sincerely sorry that she was murdered."

"You said you weren't close to Eva Keller," Rost said.

"I was close to her father. That was enough for me."

Delvaux's arrogant tone was getting on Nico's nerves, but he didn't let it show.

"And yet you helped her with her documentary," Rost said.

"You mean by getting her an appointment with someone at the bar association?" Delvaux asked, raising her eyebrows.

"For someone who says she had little or no contact with the victim, you appear to have been more interested in her work than you'd led us to believe."

"Is that why you summoned me?" she asked, visibly relieved.

"What did you imagine?" Rost said, raising his voice.

"Nothing, in fact. I didn't understand why you'd called me in."

"This video won't make it to the silver screen, Mrs. Delvaux," Nico finally said. "But we might very well end up viewing it somewhere else—in a courtroom, for example."

Nico watched as his words had the desired effect. A worried look flitted across her face, but just as quickly she pulled herself together.

"Whose idea was that appointment?" Nico asked.

"Eva asked me to help her. She knew the bâtonnier was a friend of mine. I met her when I was preparing for a role, and we got along well."

"How did Eva know?"

"I have no idea. Maybe her father mentioned it. I might have told him about that meeting."

"I thought your relationship with him was purely sexual in nature," Nico shot out.

"Yes . . . but . . ." The actress was thrown off. "We did talk from time to time, all the same. What do you think I am?"

"An excellent actress."

Marianne Delvaux didn't answer, and Nico figured she was deciding on the right demeanor to adopt. Someone knocked on the door, and Commander Théron stuck his head in, giving Delvaux a reprieve.

"Can I see you for a moment, Chief?"

Nico stood up and left the room. Théron wouldn't have bothered him for no reason.

"We just stepped on a land mine," Théron told him outside the door. "Kriven says Delvaux's son recently joined the role-playing association Mrs. Ravault belonged to, and, according to her associates, he also went to see her at her office. It's quite possible they had a fling. The lawyer liked them young."

Nico's mind was racing. That the young Delvaux had connections with two of the five victims seemed far from coincidental.

"I checked a few things. Michael Delvaux is studying law, and he's working on a master's in criminology. Mrs. Ravault could have met him in class and been intrigued by the idea of bedding the son of a famous actress. And get this: Michael Delvaux attended that 'Abuse of Truth' conference."

"Loop Becker in," Nico ordered. "I'm going back in."

Commander Maurin took Lucas Barel into custody and placed him in a cell on the fourth floor, the only one with a one-way mirror.

"I'll get them," Noumen said.

He was talking about the two students from the film school who had been working with Eva Keller. Maurin turned the hall light off so Barel couldn't see the students. It was a rudimentary setup, and Noumen required silence—the walls were paper thin.

"Never seen him before," one said.

"Me either," the other chimed in.

So Lucas Barel wasn't the student Eva Keller had fixated on. He may have come on to Etienne Delamare, but he was left-handed and wore a size 42 shoe. Nevertheless, there was the *Still Life with Lemons* mystery. They weren't finished with him, even if they now had another candidate for the man who seduced Eva Keller: Michael Delvaux.

"Did your son know Eva Keller?" Nico asked, returning to the room.

Marianne Delvaux bit her lip, no longer an actress assuming a pose. She was a mother now, and her boy was her Achilles' heel.

"What does my son have to do with this?" she asked, her voice shaky.

"Michael Delvaux's a student in criminology, right?" Nico continued. "Was it his idea to interview the bâtonnier at the bar association?"

"Absolutely not! Eva was the one who asked me. Michael hardly knew her."

"They attended the same conference at the university right before Christmas."

Delvaux seemed to be taking that in.

"Did your son know about your relationship with William Keller?"

"No. Do you think that's the sort of thing you share with your children?"

She seemed sincere and totally confused by the notion that her son could be involved in the investigation.

"Do you know a lawyer named Virginie Ravault?"

"That name means nothing to me, no."

"She was just murdered by the same man who killed Eva Keller."

"My God!"

"Your son knew her. He visited her at her office. She taught in the master's program at the Criminology Institute. What's more, Michael participated in the reenactments that were Mrs. Ravault's passion. We think they may have had a liaison."

"My poor Michael," Marianne Delvaux said, on the verge of tears.

A few minutes earlier, Nico was confident he could read her. Now he wasn't so sure. She truly deserved her César Award.

Captain Stéphane Rodon examined the suspect's perfectly cared-for teeth.

"Did you know, Mr. Barel, that you're missing two teeth?"

"Which ones?" Commander Maurin asked.

"The two upper canines, as we expected."

"What's it to you?"

"To us, not much, but to you, it means your worries have only just begun," Captain Noumen said.

"I'll call the lab." Rodon already had his phone out.

The forensics lab had taken a cast of the bite marks on Noë Valles's neck and generated a model of the perpetrator's bite.

Judge Becker was pacing. Nico had rarely seen him lose his patience like this.

"Delamare, Barel, Delvaux . . . We've got three suspects. All of them from the same school. Explain that to me. I don't get it. And I don't like it."

"To begin with, why don't you sit down," Nico said calmly. "Here's what we know: Lucas Barel used to hang out with Etienne Delamare, and even came on to him—without success. He could have tried to get back at Etienne through his cousin, Juliette. So let's go over that theory. He wears a size 42 shoe, but he could have put on overshoes that were larger. There's no sign of an Audi A3 anywhere near his residence, but that doesn't mean much. He could have borrowed one. But there's this factor as well: he's left-handed, and it's not likely that a left-handed murderer would switch to his right hand to commit a homicide. That leads me to question whether Barel's our man in Juliette Bisot's homicide."

Becker harrumphed.

"But at the same time, we have the following things to consider. He gave a Van Gogh reproduction to Etienne Delamare, *Still Life with Lemons*, and we found the name of that painting written on the wall of Virginie Ravault's bathroom. What's the connection between Barel and Mrs. Ravault? There's the conference on the abuse of truth and the fact that they probably crossed paths at the university. As for Eva Keller, the two students she was supposed to do her documentary with say Barel's not the guy they saw her with at the conference."

Becker was crossing and uncrossing his arms.

"The craziest thing is that Barel's missing two canines, and the lab will have to determine if his teeth match those of Noë Valles's killer. What's the link between Barel and Valles? So far, we don't know. And we have no link connecting Barel to Kevin Longin."

"What's the Delvaux kid doing in the middle of all this?"

"He has a motive: getting revenge for William Keller's involvement with his mother. He was registered to attend the conference, like Barel and Eva Keller. And he knew Mrs. Ravault, which means he's connected to two of the five victims. We're looking for connections to Juliette Bisot, Kevin Longin, and Noë Valles."

"If Barel's bite marks are a match, that would get Delvaux off."

"If they're a match, that would implicate Barel in at least one of the homicides, but it wouldn't necessarily mean he's responsible for all of them."

"So do you suspect a little arrangement between friends? Barel and Delvaux working together?"

"They'd have to be seriously perverse, but we have to be open to the possibility."

"Why the bite on Noë Valles's neck?"

"Why the *Still Life with Lemons*? What if they felt so superior, they couldn't refrain from leaving proud little clues—clues that could betray them in the end?"

"We'd have to prove it. Meanwhile, what's Etienne Delamare's role in all of this?" Becker was leaning forward, his hands clasped together.

"He's right-handed and wears a size 44 shoe. He goes to the same university as the other two, where he could have crossed paths with Mrs. Ravault. It's possible he's in cahoots with Barel and Delvaux. For now we shouldn't rule anything out."

"So who's the gamemaster?"

25

Rich, eccentric, talkative . . . egotistical, indifferent, emotionally disturbed, manipulative . . . He knew each one of his characteristics. He knew exactly when and how to proceed. One operation with no risks, one that he'd repeated a thousand times in his head. He had dreamed of this moment, and now it had finally come. Louis was brimming with anticipation. He would have to master his impatience and his emotions, and even his pleasure. His imitation of Vega would be perfect. If it wasn't, he'd change his approach, abandon the copycat costume, and go through with the murder his own way. There was no question of stopping. The very thought of striking with a knife, stabbing with a screwdriver, or slicing with a saw brought him to orgasm. To ecstasy.

26

Rue de la Huchette started at Place Saint-Michel and was chock-full of pedestrians checking the menus posted outside the street's restaurants. In the Middle Ages, the street had been known for its disreputable inns and pickpockets. Today it was recognized for its Greek specialties and wide-eyed tourists.

Nico and Kriven's squad walked over from their headquarters on Île de la Cité, just across the river, passing the renowned English-language bookstore Shakespeare and Company on their way. After World War I, the shop was considered the center of Paris's Anglo-American culture—at the time, it was on the Rue de l'Odéon and belonged to Sylvia Beach. Ernest Hemingway, F. Scott Fitzgerald, and James Joyce frequented it. The shop closed during World War II, but after the war, the eccentric American George Whitman opened the store at its current location. Over the years he took in thousands of aspiring writers and offered them a place to sleep in exchange for a few hours of work.

Nico, Kriven, and the rest of the team stopped in front of Michael Delvaux's building, glanced around, and entered. He lived in a loft with a view of the Seine.

"Mr. Delvaux? Police," Commander Kriven announced. "Open up." They heard muffled noises.

"If you don't open right away, we'll have to break down the door."

Kriven was toeing the line, ready to shoot the lock with a 9mmP, a Parabellum military cartridge with an ogive tip that could travel at 350 meters a second. *It's just like Kriven,* Nico thought, *to be ready to spring into action in a nanosecond.* Si vis pacem, para bellum: *if you seek peace, prepare for war.*

"I'm coming," said a male voice from the other side of the door.

Kriven lowered his weapon, as did Plassard, who was standing against the wall, next to the door. The others stepped back, and Nico waited in front of the door, his hands at his side. The lock clicked, and a tall young man opened up. His hair was mussed, and his chest was bare, exposing six-pack abs. A towel was wrapped around his waist.

"Sorry for the delay." He wore a mocking, pretentious smile.

A half-dressed young woman appeared behind him. She looked scared.

"Nobody leaves this apartment without our authorization," Nico said.

The team entered and secured the premises. The bachelor pad was quite pleasant—no surprise, given that Marianne Delvaux had the means. Judge Becker pushed his way in.

"Michael Delvaux?" Nico asked for formality's sake.

"Yes, that's me. Why the brass-band entry?"

Well, he's an insolent one, isn't he? Nico thought.

"You're half wrong, half right," Vidal answered. "We're not musically inclined, but we've got brass balls."

Delvaux shot the detective an icy glare and then sighed, as if he were granting some victory to a spoiled child.

"Sit down," Nico ordered, nodding toward the sofa.

Becker handed him a notebook.

"Please write down your contact information," Nico said, watching him take the pen. Michael was right-handed.

"Did you know Eva Keller, a student at La Fémis?" Nico asked.

"William Keller's daughter? The one who was murdered? It's all over the news. And my mother played a part in Keller's most recent movie. Did you see it?"

The son had inherited a talent for acting.

"Did you ever spend any time with Eva Keller or date her?"

"Not at all. In fact, I didn't even know that William Keller had a daughter until I saw on the news that she'd been murdered."

"So you're saying that you never met her?" Nico pressed.

"That's not true," Becker broke in. "Both of you attended the same conference right before Christmas."

"Is that so? Which one?"

"On the abuse of truth. The speakers included Virginie Ravault, with whom you had a relationship."

The mask fell from Michael Delvaux's face.

"It's true . . . I did have a liaison with Virginie. But it's been over for weeks. You may not know this, but I'm not the only student she had a fling with. She liked younger men. I'm sure she was mostly interested in me because my mother was a star. But why are we talking about Virginie? What does she have to do with Eva Keller?"

"We suspect that you murdered both of them."

"Virginie's dead? That's impossible."

"You participated in a reenactment yesterday at the Château de Versailles."

"I couldn't stay for the whole thing. I told the organizers that."

"You saw Mrs. Ravault there, playing the role of Madame de Montespan."

"Yes, but only briefly. I had a secondary role."

"What time did you leave?"

"At seven thirty. I was having dinner with my parents. Our guests can confirm that. I arrived around eight thirty, and I was there when the last guest left around one thirty in the morning."

"We'll check on that," Nico said.

"Go ahead. I'm telling the truth."

It seemed he had an alibi, but they still didn't know exactly when Virginie Ravault died.

"Then I went straight to Camille's."

"Camille's?"

"The young lady who's sitting next to me, the one you've scared half to death."

"Can you confirm that?" Becker asked, turning to the girl.

"Yes. Mick arrived around two, a bit tipsy. He collapsed on my bed and slept like a baby. We came back here this morning."

Kriven walked over to Nico and whispered in his ear, "There's no freezer or suitcase with wheels. We're still looking around."

Nico nodded.

"Did you know your mother was having an affair with William Keller?"

"That's not the kind of thing a mother usually discusses with her son. TMI."

"But you suspected that she had extramarital affairs, didn't you?" Becker asked.

"Like I said, we didn't talk much about that kind of thing. To tell the truth, we didn't talk much at all. But, in her chosen career, the temptation must have been great."

"So, her lover's daughter was murdered, and then Mrs. Ravault. Could that be purely coincidental?"

"Who knows? I'm not psychic. Spot me ten euros, and I'll go ask a fortune-teller."

"Where were you a week ago Thursday?" Nico asked.

"I went away for the long weekend."

"You left Paris?"

"I went to London on Wednesday night and came back on Sunday. It was a last-minute getaway."

"Can anyone confirm that?"

"The hotel where I stayed . . . And the girl I took with me."

Camille turned and glared at her boyfriend.

He ignored it. "I'll give you her name and phone number," he said, jotting down the information in Becker's notebook.

"And what did you do the day after you got back, on Monday?" Nico pressed, trying to pin down some connection to the Bois de Vincennes and the hotel.

"I was in class."

"And that night?"

"I was home, writing an essay. I chatted with a friend. I'll give you his name, too." He entered the information in Becker's notebook. "I imagine that you'll want to verify everything. It's like *1984*."

True enough, Nico thought. The world wasn't far removed from the one envisioned by George Orwell.

"Let's go back in time," Becker cut in. "Tell us about Sunday, May 5."

"I had lunch with my sister and her boyfriend. Afterward, he and I played a game of tennis, and I sprained my ankle. My father took me to the emergency room at four thirty in the afternoon. I didn't get out until late, the time it took to get an X-ray and see a specialist. I left the hospital around eight. My dad drove me to their place, and I spent the night with them."

"And on May 4?"

"I was home, studying for exams."

He had no alibi for the night Juliette Bisot's body was deposited in Square du Temple, but if his story was true, he was immobilized when Kevin Longin was killed.

"You need to get dressed now," Nico said. "We're going to head-quarters, where we'll see if some of Eva Keller's friends recognize you."

"That would certainly come as a surprise to me!"

"We'll see."

"Wasn't she murdered when I was in London?" Nico couldn't miss the naïve smile.

"That's true. But we still need to check some things out before we can clear you."

"I understand."

"Chief!" It was Kriven, calling from the other room. "We've got something."

Michael Delvaux tensed up.

"Plassard, keep an eye on him."

"Yes, Chief."

Nico got up and went into the other room, where Kriven and Vidal were waiting for him.

Vidal was holding a pair of slip-resistant overshoes. "Rubber soles with composite toes, made for walking in the snow and on slippery ground, adaptable to all types of shoes."

"Size 44," Kriven said.

"The six cleats look like they correspond with the prints found at Square du Temple," Nico said. "But the lab will have to confirm it."

"That said, I still don't see the relationship between Michael Delvaux and Juliette Bisot," Kriven said.

"Because there isn't one," Nico murmured, staring at the overshoes as if they were delivering a message.

27

Théron's squad had undertaken the Herculean task of going through the entire list of Criminology Institute students who had attended the "Abuse of Truth" conference. Maurin and her team were helping out. They were searching for attendees who were connected in one way or another with any of the victims, as was the case with Lucas Barel and Michael Delvaux.

"Well, damn it all to hell," Maurin said, breaking the silence.

The others all looked up at the same time.

"Listen to you, letting go a little," Théron joked.

"What did you find?" Noumen asked.

"Maybe our Oscar Wilde."

When Nico entered the commissioner's office, she and Deputy Commissioner Cohen were deep in conversation.

"Ah, Chief, there you are. Explain this mess to us."

"Virginie Ravault was the one murder too many," Cohen said. "The reporters will be at our throats."

"We're holding two suspects," Nico said. "Lucas Barel is a law student who may have murdered Noë Valles. As it turns out, Barel is missing two canines, and the lab matched his teeth to those of the killer, who left a bite mark on the victim's neck. The second suspect is Michael Delvaux, who's working on a master's degree in criminology. We have reason to believe he murdered Juliette Bisot. We discovered overshoes at his place that match the footprints found in Square du Temple. The lab confirmed it. Both men have solid alibis for the times the other victims were murdered."

"Delvaux, the actress's son! The press will have a heyday with that!" Cohen was glaring, and his jaw muscles were tight.

"What's the connection between the murderers and their victims?" Commissioner Monthalet asked.

"There isn't any, which is what makes this case so perplexing. But we were able to link Lucas Barel with Juliette Bisot and Michael Delvaux with two of the other victims, Eva Keller and Mrs. Ravault."

"What's your theory?"

"A small group of students, future criminologists seeking an adrenaline rush, get together and decide to kill the same way the masters did it, as a way of showing off what they know. When choosing their victims, they pick people who are close to them. That way they can settle their personal scores at the same time."

"Two birds, one stone," Cohen said.

"That's what I think."

"And to throw us off their scent, they exchange targets."

"Exactly."

"An organized gang," Cohen said. "Article 132-71 of the Penal Code, which means we're looking at aggravation of penalties."

Monthalet interrupted them. "Sirs, I hate to poke a hole in your theory, but you don't decide to go on a murder spree just because you're after an adrenaline high."

"You're right," Nico said. "We've got a gamemaster, too, who is skilled at manipulation and knows how to pinpoint his players' vulnerabilities. They'd have to have some serious emotional deficit or deep personality disorder to reduce their victims to nothing but objects."

"I suppose. In any case, we're still missing some of the protagonists—at least three of them," Monthalet said.

"My teams just came across a certain Oscar Van Bergh."

"Who may be our Oscar Wilde?" Cohen asked.

"We're checking. He's a law student at the Criminology Institute."

"That institute is full of frustrated students," Cohen said. "They'd rather be dealing with corpses out in the field than sitting through boring lectures."

"Our Oscar Wilde's parents live on the same floor as the Longin family. We've sent out a team to investigate."

"Interrogate the hell out of these kids," Cohen said. "I want the names of their accomplices."

Commissioner Monthalet stood up, signaling the end of the meeting. "Keep us informed, Chief. And wrap this up quickly. In the meantime, I recommend that we keep Michael Delvaux's arrest under wraps. Make it clear to his mother where her interests and those of her son lie."

"I'll make sure of it." With that, Nico left her office.

Captain Noumen politely sipped his coffee. Kevin's mother had insisted that he and Commander Maurin have something to drink and a piece of cake. How could they refuse? Kevin's brother was keeping them company in the narrow kitchen, which reeked of frying oil.

"Mrs. Longin, we've come to talk to your neighbors, the Van Bergh family," Noumen said, putting his cup down on the table.

"They're good neighbors. They help me with the little one, especially now that Kevin is . . . Well, you know."

"They have a son," Commander Maurin said softly.

"Yes, Oscar. He's a big boy now. He comes to visit his parents regularly."

"He doesn't live here anymore?"

"I think he has his own studio apartment."

"Did he and Kevin know each other?" Noumen asked.

"Of course. We moved in here when Kevin was born. Oscar was ten at the time."

"Did they get along?"

"For a long time they did. Then they had a falling out."

"What was it over?" Maurin pressed.

"Someone stole Oscar's bike from the basement, and he accused Kevin of taking it."

"But it wasn't Kevin, was it?"

"Of course not. The police picked Kevin up from time to time for fighting and tagging buildings, but he never did anything more serious than that." Mrs. Longin shrugged, and Noumen thought she looked drained. "Even though I didn't think Kevin took the bike, I offered to pay for it. But the Van Berghs wouldn't hear of it. They were very nice."

"How did Oscar react to that?"

"He was angry, which I could understand. But to tell the truth, there always seemed to be something off about him. Kevin said he saw him take a bat to a bird's nest once. And after the bike disappeared, Kevin grew afraid of Oscar."

"Did he tell you why he was afraid?"

She shrugged again.

"No, he didn't. But every time I mentioned Oscar's name, he would freeze up. I just let it go and hoped it would pass."

"Was Oscar around the weekend that Kevin died?" Maurin asked.

"I don't think so."

"How is Oscar otherwise?"

"Well, like I said, he didn't have anything to do with us after the falling out. But from what I can tell, he's quite handsome and the neighbors say he's charming. He probably has a lot of girls. But why all these questions?"

"Every detail is important," Noumen said.

"You're going to arrest the person who killed Kevin, aren't you? You promised me . . ."

Captain Noumen answered with a nod and a smile, and he and Maurin said good-bye. Back on the landing, they waited a few minutes before ringing the Van Berghs' doorbell. It was a silly strategy, however. Noumen knew that Mrs. Longin was watching through the peephole.

Nico heard her behind him.

"Knock, knock."

He swung around. Caroline was in the doorway of his office, looking pale. Since disclosing her pregnancy, Caroline had told him that the morning sickness was getting to her. But she was smiling, and for that, Nico was grateful.

"Darling, I'm so happy you're here."

"Where are you in the investigation?"

"The suspects are falling like flies. We're near the end. But I'll have a hard time getting away tonight. I know I promised you dinner . . ."

"Don't worry, I'm going home."

"I'd love for you to stay a bit. Dimitri can do without your company for a little while."

"I don't want to bother you."

"You never bother me, Caroline. Are you hungry? I could send somebody out for a croque monsieur from a little place nearby that a few of the guys found. They tell me it's pretty good."

"No, please don't!" Caroline raised her hand, indicating for him to stop. "Just the thought of it makes me sick."

Nico took her hand and kissed it. "I can't wait any longer to tell you what I need to say." He reached into his pocket and took out a box.

"What's that?"

"Open it, and you'll see."

Caroline took the box and slowly opened it.

"Nico! It's magnificent . . ."

"It's a family ring, from Odessa."

It was a gold band with a superb diamond mount. Laurel engravings flanked the jewel.

"I can't accept this."

"When I got divorced, my mother gave me this ring. She told me that life holds many surprises, and she knew I would meet the woman who was meant for me. She wanted me to keep it until I met that woman."

Caroline was trembling.

"You are the woman of my life, Caroline. I've finally found you, and I want you to wear this ring."

"I don't want you influenced by—"

"By the baby? Caroline, that sweet child will influence me my whole life. But that's not why I want you to have this. Don't you see how much I love you?"

"Yes, but . . ."

"I refuse to lose you, Caroline. And there's one thing that you must absolutely know . . ."

"Chief!" It was Rost calling him from out in the hallway. He burst into the office, stopping short when he saw Caroline.

"Oh, sorry . . . Good evening, doctor. I can come back."

"Is it important?"

"Drillan and Pons recognized our photo of Oscar Van Bergh. He's the one who picked up Eva at the conference."

"Where is he?"

"Studying at the Criminology Institute. Théron's squad is ready to go in and get him. They're awaiting your orders."

Nico hesitated, but reason won out.

"I won't be long," he told Caroline. "Can you wait? Please?"

"Of course. I won't go anywhere."

"Are you sure?"

"Don't be an idiot. Go on!" She blew him a kiss, and Nico disappeared.

The Criminology Institute was on Place du Panthéon. According to the director, Oscar Van Bergh was in the library, which was open late because exams were coming up. The director's assistant, a serious-looking young woman, met Nico, Théron, and Rost at stairwell K, and they climbed the wide carpeted steps to the top floor. The library was a narrow room with a wooden floor and a beamed ceiling. Low shelves filled with books lined the walls. The library was a rich resource in penal procedure and criminology. The copycat—or copycats—had surely been smart about using it. The students looked up from their books when Nico, Théron, and Rost walked into the room.

"Oscar Van Bergh?" Théron called out.

A few students turned their heads toward a young man sitting alone at one of the tables.

"We're arresting you for murder," Nico said, studying Van Bergh's face. He wondered if it was over now, or if the hands of the clock were bringing them inexorably closer to another victim. A victim who could die by the hand of another student in this room—a student wearing the cloak of José Vega.

28

Nico stood outside the aquariums, the holding cells near his office. They'd been dubbed the aquariums since each cell had one glass wall, so the suspects could be observed, but they couldn't interact. Delvaux was sitting on a bench with an arrogant look on his face. Maybe he thought his mother's connections would save him. Oscar Van Bergh was leaning against a graffiti-filled wall, his arms crossed. He was wearing the calm expression of someone who expected the police to apologize for their mistake. Lucas Barel was the most agitated of the three. He was chewing his fingernails and circling his cell like a fish in a bowl. Who did he kill Noë Valles for? Not for Delvaux, whose target was Keller, nor for Van Bergh, who wanted to get back at Kevin Longin for his bike. Looking at them, could anyone imagine, even for a moment, the atrocity of the crimes they had committed? How was it possible? They had angelic faces and demonic souls.

Nico walked away, leaving a uniformed officer to watch over the students. The squad room was tense. All the teams had been brought together.

"We're at a crucial point," Nico announced. "There's no margin for error. The weak link is clearly Lucas Barel, because we have irrefutable proof that he bit Noë Valles. And he looks like a pressure cooker ready to burst. We need him to give us the name of the person he killed Noë for."

Nico looked around the room, making sure everyone understood.

"We'll take another approach with Michael Delvaux: the overshoes match the prints found at Juliette Bisot's crime scene. But a good attorney can get that evidence thrown out. So we need a confession."

Kriven cracked his knuckles.

"As for Oscar Van Bergh—Eva Keller's Oscar Wilde—we know that he had a beef with Kevin Longin, although we don't know yet who killed the boy," Nico said.

Commander Maurin crossed her arms.

"And then there are the anonymous messages—all in the same handwriting and red ink—found near the bodies of Eva Keller, Noë Valles, and Virginie Ravault. The writing and the ink are identical to the writing and ink in the threats the attorney received. We need to use this lead."

"And then they'll fall like dominos," Kriven said.

"That's right. We're finally getting somewhere. We believe we have the right people in three of the homicides. But we have five victims, and we don't know who's behind the other two. Furthermore, we don't know who all the killers were doing it for."

"Do we have the gamemaster or not?" Théron asked.

"That's what we need to find out," Becker answered.

"I need to remind you that the nursery rhyme isn't finished," Nico said. "We haven't seen the 'five yummy candies' served up à la Vega. That means a sixth victim and another killer. We have to get our suspects to talk—and fast. If we must, we'll keep at it all night."

"You can count on us, Chief," Rost said.

"I want each of the three squad leaders to take one suspect. Let's get at least one of them to crack."

"If you sense an opening and need a joker, you can call Nico or me in," Becker said.

"Don't hesitate to attack their virility to destabilize them," Dominique Kreiss said.

"Okay, we know what we need to do," Nico said, concluding the meeting. "Let's push them to the breaking point!"

Caroline was leafing through a police magazine, a cup of tea by her side.

"Your secretary," she said, looking up.

Nico leaned over and kissed her. She was wearing Anya's ring.

"You had something important to tell me," she said.

He sat down across from her and took her hands in his. "Here it is. I already love this baby. Having a child with you is beyond my wildest dreams. It's the most precious gift you could ever give me. You will be the best mother, just like you already are to Dimitri."

"Have you thought about him?"

"Dimitri? He'll be crazy about the baby. That's a lock."

Nico kissed both her hands.

"Caroline, I know I've suggested in the past that one child was enough for me, but I couldn't have been more wrong. A life with you, Dimitri, and our baby is exactly what I want. When you told me you were pregnant, I was just too overwhelmed to get the right words out. I'm so sorry."

"You're sure about this?" Her eyes were brimming with tears.

"I couldn't be more sure of anything. And I don't want you to worry for even a minute about how we'll work this out. You can count on me, Caroline. And you—are you positive you want this?"

"Me?" Caroline said, surprised.

"Are you sure you want this baby?" Nico said, feeling suddenly anxious.

"I would have kept the baby no matter what, with or without you."

He pulled her close and kissed her cheek. He couldn't wait to tell his mother and his sister.

◆ ◆ ◆

Michael Delvaux watched the uniformed bootlicker who stood motionless in the room. What was he doing? Trying to compete with the guards at Buckingham Palace? Did the cops intend to let him marinate until he told them something? Who did they think he was? Ever since he was a kid, he had watched his mother put on a show. Acting was a gift she used to collect and discard lovers, a gift she used to fool his spineless father—and a gift she used to pretend she was sorry for neglecting him from the day he was born. But he had always seen through her. She had gotten serious about the director—more serious than she had ever been about her own son. Well, she wasn't the only person who could act. He knew how to follow her lead. In fact, he'd been turning in the performance of a lifetime.

The door opened, and a woman walked in and sat down across from him. A woman. Where did they get this bitch?

"I'm Commander Maurin," she said. "I have some questions for you about Eva Keller, who Oscar Van Bergh killed on your behalf. Meanwhile, you set your sights on Juliette Bisot and murdered her for Lucas Barel."

He wanted to laugh. He "set his sights on" the girl? This cop hadn't even read the police report! He'd shoved a knife into her chest, sliced up her face, and ripped out her eyes. He'd cut her into little pieces. One less broodmare for the world!

"That's a funny little arrangement you have with your friends," Maurin said.

This chick knew shit about vindication.

"Juliette was ten years old. I bet you can't get it up with a woman."

Michael balled his hands into fists. Too bad she couldn't see how hard he could get. Given the opportunity, he'd rock her world.

"We know who stole your bike, and it wasn't Kevin Longin. You really fucked up."

That was a pretty crude trap. Oscar was disappointed. Was that all these guys could come up with?

"I'm not following you, Commander . . . Péron?"

"It's Théron. But it doesn't matter what you call me. What's more interesting is that we found your name in Eva Keller's phone. How would you explain that?"

That whore had saved his number? He'd double-checked. She'd always referred to him as Wilde. There was no way they could connect her to him. This was a bullshit strategy.

"Some of Eva's friends saw you talking with her at a conference."

Okay. One point for the cops. But what else did they know that they weren't telling him? Had they found a shard from that damned bottle of Dom Pérignon—the bottle he used to knock her unconscious? A shard with his fingerprints? Impossible. He'd been meticulous about cleaning it up and getting rid of everything. But what if . . . His mind started to race. What would the gamemaster say?

"Yeah? So what if I was talking with her at the conference? Is that a crime? Hasn't that ever happened to you, Commander? You come on to a girl, and then you drop her. No explanation needed. After all, there are lots of girls out there."

"Actually, I'm the type who sees things through. Unlike you, clearly. The Keller girl wasn't just any girl. In your shoes, I would have jumped at the opportunity. No, I don't think you're capable of that. I mean, when you're with a girl for a while you have to prove yourself. Know what I'm talking about? Maybe you don't have the juice where it counts."

Eva Keller . . . She'd been sexy enough. She'd worn that dress. You could practically see through it. That dress could have given a dead man a hard-on. The cop would have to work harder to make him look like a wuss.

"Don't spend any time worrying about my cock," Oscar said, doing his best to sound nonchalant. "It's working just fine."

But this Théron was getting on his nerves.

"So, you prefer men?" the detective threw out.

Lucas Barel felt his muscles tense. He needed a fix . . . a fix of men, of rape, of murder and blood.

"Is this some kind of witch hunt?" he asked. "Are you a bunch of homophobes?"

The cop knit his brow and tightened his jaw. Lucas had struck a chord. These police gods didn't like being called intolerant. It was bad for their image.

"We have proof of your involvement in the murder of Noë Valles."

Okay, he bit him. That was the least of it, of course. The stinking little rat had fallen right into his trap. It had been almost too easy. He'd taken such pleasure in watching the kid bleed out and then eating his flesh. The gamemaster had wanted him to imitate Fritz Haarmann. What did he care, as long as he got his fix. There'd been one slipup, though. He'd forgotten to tell Louis that he was missing his two canine teeth, a distinguishing mark. The gamemaster would be pissed off when he found out.

"We also know that you're linked to the murder of Mrs. Ravault."

"Excuse me?" Lucas sat up straight.

"That should be 'Excuse me, Commander Kriven.' Now, tell me: Does *Still Life with Lemons* mean anything to you?"

He'd given it to Etienne in memory of their weekend in Louviers. Etienne had let him touch him. Etienne was smart, and he smelled good. He was no prey. He could have been a partner. But Etienne had made it clear . . .

"We found those words above Mrs. Ravault's body. And the message 'three round coins' written in the same ink next to Noë Valles. What do you have to say for yourself? You're in a tight spot here, Barel."

Why make Van Gogh's painting part of the Acid Bath Killer's crime scene, other than to echo the "four planes a pretty lemon yellow" in the nursery rhyme? Was it a trap—a way of getting rid of him? Of throwing him to the wolves?

"*Still Life with Lemons:* you either used it yourself or told your friend who killed Mrs. Ravault about it."

The cop didn't get it at all. Lucas had to remain calm. He had to stay strong.

"Just so you know, Michael Delvaux is ratting you out right now. He admitted to killing Juliette Bisot, and he said you had him do it."

Why use the Van Gogh? He'd get life for Noë Valles in any case—but for the others, too?

The cop leaned across the table. He was handsome . . . the dark and swarthy type. His gaze pierced him like an arrow.

"Do you want to be the only one to pay for Noë Valles's murder? We know you killed him for someone else. And it wasn't for Delvaux or Van Bergh. So who was it for? Who asked you to kill Noë Valles?"

"It was to honor Fritz Haarmann!" Lucas spit out.

"Who told you that Valles was ideal prey? The kind that Haarmann would have chosen? You had suggested Juliette Bisot, to be killed à la Chikatilo, and Michael Delvaux did the dirty work. Who gave you Noë Valles's name? Who?"

Lucas could feel the blood pulsing in his brain. The walls were closing in. Now he was the rat. But these cops had it all wrong. None of them had the imagination or the intellect to carry out a scheme like theirs. Only a superior species could achieve what they had done. These guys were just ordinary flatfoots—except this one.

"Who gave you the name?" the cop shouted, just inches from his face.

Too close. Lucas cried out in rage as he planted his lips on the cop's. The reaction was immediate: the uniformed officer jumped him and pulled him away, and the detective punched him in the gut. He doubled over, hardly able to breathe. That damn whore Valles! He had been willing to do anything for food and a place to sleep. And Juliette? He didn't give a shit about her. This cop was a thousand miles from the truth. But that bitch Ravault . . . She had humiliated him. She had treated him like half a man because he was a homosexual. Louis had avenged him. Louis had loved him!

"Louis!" he barked victoriously.

The room fell silent. The uniformed officer picked him up by the collar and handcuffed him.

"Louis?" the detective asked. "Louis had something against Noë Valles?"

So this cop was a dumbass, too.

"Alban Lancia," he said, exhausted.

29

"Alban Lancia, twenty-two years old, another student at the Criminology Institute," Captain Plassard said. He looked tired. "Alban's mother married Noë Valles's father when he was ten. It was all downhill from there. Noë's chronic instability, which ran the gamut from self-mutilation to attempted suicide, sucked all the air out of the family and left Alban with nothing. Noë was hospitalized on a number of occasions, which did give Alban a few moments of peace. But then Noë would come back and deplete the family again. The drugs and the prostitution came afterward."

"So that was the score Alban wanted to settle," said Becker, who was slumped in an armchair. "We need to arrest him. Did Barel say who Lancia's victim was? Was it Longin or Ravault?"

"Not yet," Plassard answered. "Kriven's working him right now."

"He should keep at him and not let up," Nico said.

Plassard nodded. "So here's another piece of news: Alban Lancia drives an Audi A3."

"Which he lent to Michael Delvaux?" Becker asked.

"We'll have to check, but it would seem that he did. There's something off with the Bisot case, though."

"Why wouldn't Barel have killed Etienne Delamare instead of his cousin?" Nico said.

"Malignant narcissism suggests someone who satisfies his desires and urges at the expense of others, whom he manipulates," Becker said.

"I see that Dominique Kreiss's lessons have been effective," Plassard said.

Becker smiled. "Only fools never change their minds."

"There's a detail we should keep in mind: Louis," Nico said.

"Why did Lucas Barel use that name when he was accusing Alban Lancia?" Becker asked.

"What if Louis is the gamemaster?" Nico suggested.

"That would explain Barel's blunder. Ask Kriven to pound away on this Louis thing," Becker said. "We need to know who he is. And arrest Alban Lancia right away."

Alban ran and ran until his lungs felt like they were being ripped out of his chest. The hoarse sound of his breathing echoed in his head, and his belly hurt. He could hear them catching up to him. He was afraid . . . But the murder was justified. He had imagined killing Noë with his own hands a thousand times. But in the end, the exercise had given him even more pleasure. Kevin . . . Getting to know the kid over a period of several weeks without being noticed, luring him into a deserted classroom to smoke a joint, his butcher's knife sharpened like a master chef's . . .

They were closing in. He ran faster. His lungs burned. He couldn't outrun them. Alban would tell them. He would tell them about the hell he had endured with Noë.

He felt a hand on his shoulder. He tripped. A man jumped on top of him, tackling him. A cop . . .

Nico knocked and walked in. Kriven started to stand up.

"No, that's unnecessary, Commander."

Nico grabbed a chair and set it down near Lucas Barel. Something wasn't right.

"I'm chief of the Criminal Investigation Division," he said. "Thanks to you, we've arrested Alban Lancia. Louis is now the only one who's still free . . ."

Kriven had been at it for hours, but Lucas hadn't given Louis up. Maurin and Théron were applying pressure to Michael Delvaux and Oscar Van Bergh, but they hadn't offered up the slightest clue, either. They were all protecting the gamemaster. Nico was sure of it. Louis was their leader, and lowlifes took loyalty seriously, because it was strengthened by fear. They needed another approach. Delvaux got his revenge through Eva Keller. Van Bergh gave up Kevin Longin, and Alban Lancia wiped Noë Valles from his life. But was it Lucas Barel or Louis who had been after Virginie Ravault? And what about Juliette Bisot?

"Etienne Delamare rejected you, despite that promising weekend in Louviers," Nico said.

"Juliette dovetailed perfectly with the profile of Andrei Chikatilo's victims," Kriven said. "So you used her to get revenge on Etienne."

Lucas's face flushed with anger. Nico could see that he was at the mercy of an incendiary mix of contradictory emotions. If he kept fighting them, he'd explode.

"I didn't give a shit about that girl!" Lucas howled.

"Who provoked you? Who humiliated you to the point of deserving a good lesson?" Nico thundered.

"That slut laughed at me! Told me I was useless. And she was an expert at sex, that's for sure."

"Who? Mrs. Ravault?"

Lucas closed up like an oyster. Nico rose from his chair and nodded to Kriven, indicating they should step outside.

"What do you think?" Kriven asked once they were in the hallway.

"Come with me."

They headed off to Nico's office, where Caroline had fallen asleep.

"Oh," Kriven said. "What happened?"

"We were supposed to go out for dinner," Nico said.

"What exactly are you looking for?"

Caroline woke up and stretched like a cat.

"Hello, doctor," Kriven said.

"Hello. So where do things stand?" There was no sign of impatience in her voice, just genuine interest.

"The chief was just about to share one of his flashes of insight."

"Kriven, don't get started," Nico warned, going through his papers.

Caroline giggled, and Nico felt like he was sprouting wings.

"Voilà! I knew I'd seen it somewhere."

Caroline stood up.

"Etienne Louis Delamare."

"So Delamare is Louis?" Kriven asked.

"Who else would have wanted to kill Juliette Bisot? Who had no motive in Mrs. Ravault's killing, nor any connection to her? Who knew about *Still Life with Lemons*?"

"Delamare."

"He's the only one I can see. He played the victim when he was undoubtedly the gamemaster."

"Why have Juliette killed?"

"Because he hated his uncle? Because he was jealous of his aunt? Because he couldn't stand his stepcousin Juliette, an outsider to the family? We're going to ask him."

He looked at Caroline. "We're almost there, sweetheart. I'll have an officer take you home. You need your sleep."

Someone rang the bell and then banged on the door. It was 2:53 in the morning. They were going to wake up the whole building, but there was no need. He had been waiting for them. Louis had predicted their arrival, and Louis's word was sacred. Their carefully assembled structure was collapsing like a house of cards. It was his fault; he hadn't been vigilant enough, and he had to be punished. Louis had said so.

"This is Chief Sirsky. Open up." The voice was calm, determined.

He could provoke them, force them to shoot. But did he really want that?

"We'll break down the door if we have to."

"I'm coming."

"Do you have a weapon?" somebody else asked.

A comedian. He didn't bother replying and unlocked the door. Several men, guns in hand, stood ready to shoot.

"Etienne Delamare?" the chief asked.

He trembled. The man had already been here, so why was he asking?

"Etienne *Louis* Delamare?"

He felt dizzy. Nauseated.

"Louis, the gamemaster?"

The gamemaster . . . He came back to himself.

"Yes! It's me," he declared, full of pride.

30

"I just filled the commissioner in. That's quite a hand you played," Cohen thundered, all jolly and enjoying a smoke next to his open window.

"We still have some loose ends to tie up," Nico said.

"Formalities, right? Let me know when you've crossed the finish line. I'm not going anywhere this morning." Cohen gave Nico a salute, and Nico got up and left his boss's office.

8:45 a.m. Thirteen days earlier, they had discovered the lifeless body of Juliette Bisot. A little girl like so many others, who had loved ballerinas and tutus and playing princess. What if Caroline was having a girl? Would she like to dance, too? Would he have to worry about her? Would he have to watch for predators? Predators who could be anyone, even law and criminology students who seemed upstanding in every way.

"He's here," Nico's secretary said.

Nico welcomed the man into his office.

"Mr. Bisot. Please sit down."

"Why did you summon me?" Juliette's stepfather asked, looking suspicious.

"We arrested your daughter's murderer," Nico said as gently as possible.

The man slumped in his chair, covered his face with his hands, and wept. Nico felt his heart tighten.

"Who was it? Why did he do it?"

"It's a complicated story, which, I'm sorry to say, will be another hard blow."

"I don't understand."

"Your nephew Etienne is an accomplice in Juliette's murder."

"An accomplice? That's impossible!"

The man's face flushed with anger. The news was clearly too much for him. Nico explained, knowing he had to be quick or Juliette's father would lose it.

"How will I ever be able to tell my wife? And my sister will never accept it! My family is ruined."

He was sobbing now. Snot dripped from his nose, and he did nothing to stop it.

"Sir, please try to calm yourself, or I'll have to call the paramedics. Your blood pressure must be skyrocketing."

Eventually the sobs became muted. Juliette's father wiped his nose and looked up.

"The bastard," he said through clenched teeth. "I'll kill him with my own hands. And the one who hurt my little girl . . . my little princess."

The five students had ended up confessing. The scandal would break the next day: a real-life murder party with a celebrity's son in the mix.

"He used the name Louis . . ."

"Louis?"

For a fraction of a second, Nico saw contradictory feelings on the man's face: surprise, disgust, and anger.

"Why do you think he did that?"

"It's his middle name," Bisot said.

"Did he use it often?"

"Not that I know of."

The man had once again assumed a mask of pain.

"Where does that middle name come from?" Nico suddenly asked.

"His maternal grandfather . . . My father."

Etienne Delamare had named the killer who inhabited him Louis. But why?

"What was their connection?"

"Etienne was little when he died. I don't even know if he remembers him. My God . . . Juliette."

Nico called his secretary, who arranged to have an officer drive Mr. Bisot to an emergency room. He was worried that the man might have a stroke or a heart attack. Better to have a doctor take a look. Now Nico had one more promise to keep. It was to William Keller.

Nico admired the cloudless blue sky as he left police headquarters. He loosened his tie and hit "Play." The compelling voice of Serge Gainsbourg filled the car. He was singing about heartbreak, love, and boomerangs, a song that could have been about Caroline and himself. A few days ago he had been heartsick over the prospect of losing her. Today he was giddy with love.

He turned the volume down and called his mother.

"Mom?"

"Nico! I've been hoping you'd call."

"Work's been busy."

"So I gathered. I heard it on the news. And how are things with Caroline? Did you manage to talk to her?"

"Yes, and I have some great news."

"I knew it! Tanya told me she was pale and didn't eat a bite when they had lunch together."

Nico grinned. Anya was so smart. She had seen what was right before his eyes even when he had been totally oblivious.

"I gave her the ring, Mom."

There was a pause. "I knew that ring would go to her one day," Anya finally said. "She's always been the one."

He ended the call and spotted the sign for Saint-Germain-en-Laye, where Eva Keller's parents lived. Nico felt the weight of the news he was about to deliver. William would soon have to come to terms with his role in what had happened. Delvaux's mental illness and criminal nature wouldn't matter. It was William's relationship with Marianne that had triggered the chain reaction. Without it, Eva would still be alive today.

Nico heard Gainsbourg's voice again in the background: "If . . . I shoot myself, it will be because of you."

Nico slammed on the brakes and pulled off the road. He could feel the blood pounding in his temples, and he felt like he was drowning. He was sucking in water. *Don't panic. Concentrate. Relax.* He took a few deep breaths. Then he started the car again and turned around. Keller would have to wait. He reached his secretary.

"What hospital was Juliette Bisot's father taken to?"

"I'll find out, Chief."

"Put Commander Maurin on."

"Right away."

There were a few clicks.

"Yes, Chief?"

"Do you have your notes on Juliette Bisot?"

"Right here."

"Can you check our family information for Martin Bisot's father?"

"Here it is. Louis Marie Joseph Bisot. Two children: Martin, Juliette's stepfather; and France, the eldest, Etienne Delamare's mother. Annie Bisot, his widow, is still alive."

"Where is she?"

"She lives in Louviers."

"Hold on, Maurin. I've got another call."

"Chief? Martin Bisot can't be found. He left the hospital without telling anyone."

"Good God. Thanks for telling me. Maurin? You still there?"

"Yes, Chief. What is it?"

"I'll give you fifteen minutes to meet me at the Porte d'Auteuil with a member of your team. Bring Becker, too. I'll explain on the way. I'll need the case file. Hurry!"

Nico turned on his siren and left a message for Kriven.

Becker sat in front. Maurin and Noumen were in the back.

"So, you're taking us to Normandy?"

"Martin Bisot's disappeared. I told the local police to put out an all-points bulletin on him. Maurin, what's the name on Martin Bisot's birth certificate?"

"Martin Louis Bisot."

"What are you thinking?" Becker asked. He was clutching the roof handle, as the car was going very fast. Careening, in fact.

"When I mentioned the name Louis, Bisot tensed up, and his face changed. The pain left his eyes, and I saw something deeper and violent. It wasn't about Juliette anymore. It was as if I saw his real face for the first time. And when he told me the origin of the name Louis, I saw fear."

"That doesn't sound like enough to call in the cavalry."

"I have more: castles, a tree, a boat, and a bull. I mean . . . I think . . ."

His phone rang. It was Kriven. He hit speakerphone.

"You're right! It's the emblem of the University of Cantabria: an oak tree, a boat on three waves, and an Altamira bison—a cave painting from a grotto that bears the name. They're surrounded by four golden castles. During her studies, Dr. Bisot spent some time at the Marqués de Valdecilla Hospital in Santander, which is part of the university. She and Martin spent their honeymoon there."

Becker whistled. "And where did you see the emblem?" he asked.

"Around Dr. Bisot's neck when they identified their daughter at the morgue."

"I was there, and I can confirm what the chief saw," Kriven said over the phone.

"That brings us back to Santander," Nico said. "To José Vega and the sixth victim."

"The link between the Bisot family and Santander has been established, a connection that Etienne Delamare must have been aware of as gamemaster," Becker said.

"Etienne Delamare doesn't have the makings of a gamemaster. He'd like to be one, but he isn't. Rost, are you there?"

"Yep," Rost answered over the speaker.

"Why Louis? That's the knot I need to unravel. Call back when you have something."

They sped along the highway that linked Paris to Caen. Destination: Normandy and Louviers, a name from the Latin word *luparia*, "a place haunted by wolves."

The family home, a sprawling plot of perfectly maintained land, was a five-minute walk from downtown. Dr. Bisot opened the door, looking dumbfounded. They walked in without giving her time to gather her wits, and Maurin and Noumen started their search.

"Take us to the back," Nico ordered.

She led them, trembling as she walked. The kitchen had a door to the backyard. She had been preparing lunch.

"Where's my husband?" she asked.

"He left Paris, but he should be here soon."

"He was in Paris?"

"I called him in to headquarters this morning."

"But why?"

"Before I explain, we have a few questions for you, Dr. Bisot."

"Of course. I'm listening."

"What kind of relationship did your husband have with his father, Louis Bisot?"

"Louis? From what I know they didn't get along very well."

"Do you know why?" Becker asked.

"What's the point of digging up the past? Martin doesn't like to talk about it."

The detectives had found a black hole: Martin Bisot had missed an entire year of school. He was twelve at the time. The lapse had been uncovered during the initial investigation of his stepdaughter's disappearance, but it hadn't seemed important at the time.

"It's never easy for a victim to confide in others," Nico said.

The blood drained from Dr. Bisot's face.

"What happened to him?" Becker pressed.

"From what I know, Martin was sexually abused as a child," she said.

"By his father?"

The make-or-break question.

"Yes, what happened to him was awful. His father stopped when he got older and sent him to boarding school in Switzerland."

It was a textbook case: when the boy's voice changed and his chest started sprouting hair, he no longer pleased Louis Bisot. So the father sent the son away for a full year to make him understand that their intimate relationship was over. What had gone on in the adolescent's head during that time? Once he returned home, contradictory feelings of relief, hate, and rejection had probably eaten away at him. Perverse as it was, he may even have regretted that his father was no longer lavishing attention on him.

"And his mother? What part did she play in all of this?" Nico asked.

"She denied it. I tried to talk to her about it once, but she just got angry. She said Martin had invented the whole story, that he had psychological problems."

"How did Martin behave with Etienne?" Becker asked.

"He was Martin's only nephew. Martin loved him. Our son came along much later."

"Did they spend time together?"

"Yes, of course, but . . ."

"Etienne used the name Louis. Why is that name so significant to him?"

"My husband's middle name is Louis, and they used to play what they called the Louis game."

"What kind of game?" Becker asked.

"Well, they played the king and his dauphin, something like that."

So that was it. All this time, Etienne had been eager to succeed the king. That was why he was so quick to claim he was gamemaster when he was arrested. He *wanted* to be the gamemaster. But the king was not dead, and Etienne was just a valet, someone who followed the king's orders. And the saddest part of all: Martin Bisot had probably defiled his nephew for years, forming a sordid bond between victim and torturer.

The question remained as to why Martin Bisot had switched to murder. What had triggered the onslaught of violence? What important life event had prompted this psychopath to act out? Had it been the birth of his own biological child? Did his stepdaughter no longer belong in the family portrait? Had he decided to push her out to create the perfect family with no child by another man? What kind of twisted thinking was that? Nico shuddered.

Right now, however, there was a more urgent question.

"Where does your mother-in-law live?" he asked, his tone full of authority.

Seventy-four-year-old Annie Bisot was the next victim on the list, Nico was sure of it. She would be raped and smothered—killed à la José Vega. Martin Bisot had to hate Spain and Santander, the symbols of a sham marriage and family that he had bought into but never embraced. His childhood family had long ago made him a psychopathic killer with a perverse agenda.

Judge Becker stayed in the car while reinforcements surrounded the cozy home. Noumen nodded, and they crept in closer. Muffled sounds were coming from the second floor, and they rushed in, with Maurin protecting their backs.

"No!" a woman cried out.

Nico glanced at Noumen and donned his invisible armor. Noumen shoved the bedroom door open, and Nico rushed in, with Maurin on his heels. Martin was leaning over his mother, her ice-blue nightgown bunched around her waist. She turned her head toward Nico, a pleading look in her eyes.

"Police!" Nico shouted.

Martin let go of his mother and stood up, his eyes filled with incandescent rage and a trail of spittle hanging from his lips. He looked like a famished wolf interrupted in the middle of a meal. As his mother shrieked, Martin dove behind the bed. Nico followed, landing on the suspect's back, splaying him, and knocking his gun out of his hand. Maurin rushed over and kicked the weapon across the room. Nico grabbed the man's arm and elbow-locked him. Noumen cuffed him.

Now Martin Bisot was nothing more than a pathetic little boy, his hands behind his back, his glazed eyes on the cabbage-rose rug beneath his feet. Nico looked at him and shook his head.

"Game over, Martin."

31

"Congratulations, Chief," Commissioner Monthalet said through the speakerphone. "I believe it's over now."

"The investigation is closed. Now it's up to the justice system."

"You and Judge Becker make quite a pair."

They heard Cohen's laugh echo in the car, which they were driving back to Paris, carrying the suitcase that had been used to transport little Juliette.

"It's no good for promotions. We know all about that, don't we, Commissioner?"

"Don't listen to him, Chief," Monthalet said, serious, as usual. "Again, congratulations. Drive carefully."

Nico smiled, turned on the siren and flashing lights, and pressed on the accelerator.

Becker grabbed the roof handle again. "Would you tell us, once and for all, why you think you're Superman? Why you're acting like bullets can't hurt you?"

Nico just grinned.

"So, spill the beans."

Even though his friend was teasing him, Nico could tell he was worried. He looked in the rearview mirror and saw Maurin and Noumen pretending not to listen.

"I'm luckier than Superman ever was. I'm going to be a dad again!"

There was a long silence. Noumen was the first to break it with an ear-busting whoop. He high-fived Maurin.

Becker put a hand on his shoulder. "Caroline is pregnant?"

"That's exactly what I said, *Monsieur le Juge.*"

"We needed some good news. And this is the best," Becker said. "Let me know when you want to put the crib together. I'll be right over."

Nico grinned as he saw himself rocking his baby to sleep. And another folk song came to him. It was one Anya had sung to Dimitri.

> *The dream passes by the window,*
> *And sleep by the fence.*
> *The dream asks sleep,*
> *"Where shall we spend the night?"*

> *Where the cottage is warm,*
> *Where the baby is tiny,*
> *There we will go,*
> *And rock the child to sleep.*

He couldn't wait to get home.

ABOUT THE AUTHOR

Writing has always been a passion for Frédérique Molay, author of the award-winning, internationally bestselling Paris Homicide series. She graduated from France's prestigious Sciences Po and began her career in politics and French government administration. She worked as chief of staff for the French National Assembly and then worked for the local government in Burgundy, ran in the European elections, and was elected in Saône-et-Loire.

Meanwhile, she spent her nights pursuing a passion for writing she'd nourished since she wrote her first novel at the age of eleven. At the height of her brilliant political career, Molay won France's prestigious crime fiction award, the Prix du Quai des Orfèvres, for *The 7th Woman*. She took a break from politics to continue the series and raise her three children.

Looking to the Woods is the fourth book in the Paris Homicide mystery series, featuring chief of police Nico Sirsky. Molay is currently at work on the fifth. Her passion for her career never left her, so she returned to politics as chief of staff for a senator. She now splits her time between Paris and Burgundy, between police procedurals and politics.

ABOUT THE TRANSLATOR

Anne Trager loves France so much she has lived there for more than a quarter of a century and just can't seem to leave. What keeps her there is a uniquely French mix of pleasure seeking and creativity. After many years working in translation, publishing, and communications, she woke up one morning and said, "I just can't stand it anymore. There are way too many good books being written in France not reaching a broader audience." That's when she founded Le French Book in order to translate and publish some of those works in English. The company's motto is "If we love it, we translate it," and Trager loves crime fiction, mysteries, and detective novels.

Made in the USA
San Bernardino, CA
20 February 2017